'Why did you  **me, Paris?'**

'Why?' she echoe

'Yes, why? Because I'm famous?'

'Famous? Don't be absurd. And I already told you after we—in the—I already told you I wasn't like that!'

'Then why the regret?'

'I don't *believe* you!' she exclaimed tearfully. 'How can you even *ask* me that? Why are you *being* like this?'

'Because I'm beginning to wonder if I haven't been used,' he said quietly.

Dear Reader

What a great selection of romances we have in store for you this month—we think you'll love them! How about a story of love and passion, set in the glamorous world of the movies—with deception and double-dealing to thrill you? Or perhaps you'd prefer a romance with the added spice of revenge . . .? We can offer you all this and more! And, with exotic locations such as Egypt, Costa Rica and the South Pacific to choose from, your only problem will be deciding which of our exciting books to read first!

The Editor

Emma Richmond was born during the war in north Kent when, she says, 'Farms were the norm and motorways non-existent. My childhood was one of warmth and adventure. Amiable and disorganised, I'm married with three daughters, all of whom have fled the nest— probably out of exasperation! The dog stayed, reluctantly. I'm an avid reader, a compulsive writer and a besotted new granny. I love life and my world of dreams, and all I need to make things complete is a housekeeper— like, yesterday!'

A
WAYWARD LOVE

BY
EMMA RICHMOND

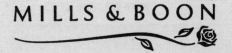

MILLS & BOON LIMITED
ETON HOUSE, 18-24 PARADISE ROAD
RICHMOND, SURREY TW9 1SR

*MILLS & BOON and the Rose Device
are trademarks of the publisher.*

*First published in Great Britain 1994
by Mills & Boon Limited*

© Emma Richmond 1994

*Australian copyright 1994   Philippine copyright 1994
This edition 1994*

ISBN 0 263 78696 X

*Set in Times Roman 10 on 12 pt.
01-9410-52213 C*

Made and printed in Great Britain

CHAPTER ONE

'AMBIENT enough for you, is it?'

He ignored her, continued to inspect the stone hut that huddled miserably beside the fast-running river. A bit like herself. She was cold, wet, her boots leaked, and the last thing she needed was to be stuck here in the middle of nowhere with Oliver Darke, famous actor. He was impatient, irritable, sarcastic, cynical, and probably believed his own publicity. He was also disturbing, and that made her cross.

For the past two weeks she'd been running around in ever decreasing circles, with Oliver Darke causing most of the confusion, because the Great Actor expected to be pandered to, his nose wiped, his ego soothed... 'You *are* being paid, Paris.' Yes. Inadequately, in her opinion... Stop grouching. With a rather wry smile, she leaned in the crumbling doorway, examined his tall, lithe figure as he continued to stand with his eyes unfocused, his hands hanging limp at his sides, and tried to be impartial. He was a good actor, a superb actor. Charismatic, her sister would have said. Excellent presence. But then, she would have said that, wouldn't she? Her sister *liked* actors.

Hearing the car door slam, she turned to see what Henry was up to. Henry, dressed all in black, who looked as though he yearned to leap on any passing funeral procession. Oliver's dresser, gofer, odd job man, and minder. Henry, who thought he was coming down with flu.

With a heartfelt sigh, she straightened. 'Don't be long,' she warned Oliver. In her experience, the only way to cope with the acting profession was to behave like Monster Nanny, otherwise nothing ever got done. Leaving him with his ambience, she walked back towards the cold comfort of the car. Tall and thin—slim, she mentally corrected, one had to have a bit of self worth in this life—an ordinary-looking girl. Average looks, average shape, average intelligence. Dark hair with a slight curl, and amused blue eyes. *Usually* amused blue eyes; life at the moment hadn't given her very much to be amused about. But she dressed well, she thought with a rather humorous defiance. Always. Bought the best she could afford; she just wished someone had thought to tell her that they would be filming in mud.

'Oliver nearly ready?' Henry asked hopefully. His voice had developed a theatrical croak.

'I've no idea.'

'And you've spoken with the villagers?'

'I have.'

'And they won't be a problem?'

'No.'

'You impressed upon them the need to keep the area clear? Not to intrude when we return with the rest of the crew?'

'I did.'

'Good. And Oliver's happy with the location?'

'I don't know. I didn't ask him.'

Irritability was catching. Grimacing an apology, she patted his shoulder, wished there were someone to pat hers, opened the car door and climbed thankfully inside. Huddled into her mac, she stared gloomily through the windscreen. Being an interpreter wasn't always a bed of roses. 'Take Oliver and Henry to look at the new location,' the director had said. 'Have a quick word with the villagers, then back before lunch.' Hah. The roads had been slippery with water and debris due to the dismal weather that had been blanketing Europe for the past few weeks; the owner of the field had been away in Oporto; Henry thought he was getting flu, and Oliver Darke, famous actor, was in a foul mood. Great. And you're being extraordinarily bitchy, Paris. Yes. Not really wanting to consider her own behaviour, she switched on the ignition and turned the heater up to full blast.

Five minutes later, Oliver began trudging up the rain-slick field. Even wet, and in a temper, he was impossibly good-looking. Loose-limbed, long legged, with heavy-lidded dark brown eyes. Unbelievably sexy. He could adopt a smouldering look at will, and usually did. Dark blond hair, probably dyed, she assured herself. The even white teeth probably owed more to an orthodontist than nature, and the rugged chin to the art of a plastic surgeon, and he was probably not used to pigging it in a small car in the middle of Portugal's Costa Verde in the worst weather imaginable. Which was a pity, because the scenery, when it could be seen, was exquisite.

The rear door was snatched open and both men got in. 'Let's go,' Oliver said shortly.

Thrusting the hired car into drive, she slowly negotiated the slippery field and edged on to the track. Dark clouds appeared to tangle with the trees, that dripped; the windscreen wipers squeaked; Henry sounded as though he was conducting an experiment with his sinuses; and Oliver was extremely silent. Grimly so, one might say.

'How long?' he asked abruptly.

'The same as out. Half an hour.' Maybe. If she didn't get lost, managed to find the right track.

'Something is amusing you?' he drawled.

Quite unaware that she'd been smiling, she flicked her eyes up to the rear-view mirror, then quickly away again. 'No,' she murmured. Whatever else Oliver Darke might do, he didn't amuse her. Thankfully seeing the sign for Espinho, she turned on to the right road, and a silent thirty minutes later they arrived on the set.

George, the director, hurried over with flattering promptness, opened the door, helped his star out and escorted him towards the large white trailers that sat in a wagon-train-like circle on the edge of the field. Henry hurried behind like a downtrodden puppy. Eager, but ill.

Climbing out, she turned to survey the scene of utter chaos that confronted her. She didn't know much about film-making but she had always assumed it was a little more organised than this. Of course the rain didn't help, turning everything to mud as it had. She had also assumed that film-making involved far more people than those spread out before her. And where was the director's chair? she wondered. They *always* had a director's chair! There were cameramen, various technicians, lighting and sound experts, and a continuity man, who was leaning back against a tree with an expression of profound boredom on his face.

Moving her eyes towards the other side of the small field, she watched entranced as a young girl dressed in period costume threw a tantrum, and a tall, slim man dressed in the tattered uniform of one of Wellington's troops, artistically daubed in blood, shouted back.

'It's muddy!'

'Of course it's muddy! It's been bloody raining for weeks!'

'Well, there's nothing in my contract that says I have to crawl through mud!'

'There's nothing in your contract that says you have to throw a tantrum every five minutes either! You're supposed to be the intrepid heroine, for God's sake, not a shrinking violet who needs her bloody hand held every five minutes!' Turning on his very muddy heel, he stalked back up the field.

Tempers were obviously getting frayed, nerves stretched; they were way over budget, and time was running out. Everything normal, in fact.

Turning up the collar of her raincoat, Paris picked her way towards the action and met him halfway.

'You took your time!' he grouched irritably.

'Yes.'

'Hmph.' Obviously unable to think of anything else to accuse her of, he turned his attention elsewhere, saw the tubby director, and yelled across to him. 'George! I'm going to have a drink!' Without waiting for a reply, he stalked across to one of the smaller trailers and disappeared inside. Enter and exit unknown actor. Oliver's stand-in. The one who did the boring bits—and got shouted at by the exciting new starlet, Melissa Bright.

Amused by the exchange, because it was, after all, what she expected from actors, she continued on her way. Halting beside George, for whom she'd been working for all of three weeks, and wished she wasn't, she asked amiably, 'Alcoholic, is he?'

Turning a startled face towards her, he demanded blankly, 'What?'

'Actor chummy,' she explained with a little movement of her head towards the trailer.

'Alcoholic? Of course he isn't!' he snapped with the same sort of irritability as the soldier. 'And I expected you back hours ago!'

'Sorry,' she apologised absently as her attention was diverted towards the young actress who was flouncing, as well as anyone could flounce through mud, although she was making a pretty good stab at it, towards her own trailer, her skirts held high above her knees. When she reached the comparative safety of the top step, she turned to make a last dramatic statement.

'And I'm warning you, George, if you don't get that imbecile to change his attitude, I shall walk off the set! The man's an absolute pig.'

George sighed.

'Always like this, is it?' Paris asked commiseratingly.

'Yes. No. If it would only stop *raining*! And if she carries on her bad temper with Oliver...'

Not being able to do much about the weather, only the language, and perhaps trying to make up for her own bad mood, she asked, kindly, 'Want me to have a word?'

'Would you?' he asked gratefully.

'Sure.' For some reason she was the only one who could get anywhere near the temperamental young actress. Probably because she didn't offer competition.

'Thanks, Paris.' With a faint smile that looked very forced, he added, 'Then you'd best get yourself a cup of tea while there's still time.' With another sigh, he lumbered across to have a word with the cameraman.

Passing one of the technicians, who smiled at her then gave a comical shrug, she grinned, and continued on to Melissa's caravan. Ten minutes later, her duty done, although not very nicely, she had to admit, she hurried across to the tea-wagon. Much to her surprise, Oliver was sitting on one of the long bench seats, legs thrust out before him, a cup nursed in his palms. He was already changed into his soldier's uniform, mud, blood, and God knew what else daubed about his person, and the dark wig he was to wear, which was perched like a dead hedgehog beside him, somehow managed to look the most contented thing she'd seen all week.

While she made her tea and something to eat, she watched him from the corner of her eye. Impatient, restless, moody, she decided—and bloodstained, of course. 'All ready for the off?' she asked lightly.

'Perceptive,' he muttered rudely.

With a little shrug, knowing that he liked her even less than she liked him, she continued to fill the silences that tended to stretch between them. 'Doesn't look the sort of epic you'd want to be involved in.'

'Doesn't it?'

'No.' Not that she knew very much about him, only what she'd read in the Press; although she wasn't daft enough to believe everything she read, stories were usually *based* on fact, and there had been that rather nasty piece about the way he'd treated a young girl not so long ago, and, whether true or not, her own observations about his character this past week hadn't yet given her any reason to dismiss such allegations out of hand, or change her mind about him. But his private life aside, in the one or two films she had seen him in he'd been either a hard-hitting industrialist, or a cop. Meaty script, tough action. Nothing at all like this. 'Docudrama, isn't it?'

Still staring moodily down into his cup, he gave a brief, unamused laugh. 'One word for it. I certainly can't fault the drama.'

'No. Always difficult, is she? Melissa?'

'So I believe.'

'But the producers would only agree to fund the production if Melissa was in it? Because she's flavour of the month?' But obviously not his month, judging by his scowl. She was supposed to be portraying Isabella Soares, a Portuguese girl who followed the drum, and her lover, Captain Richard Marsh, as portrayed by Oliver, who was wounded at Almeida and captured by the French. She rescued him, dragged him across country, and eventually took him to the stone hut they'd just viewed. 'And I never did discover how she got him this far,' she commented musingly.

'Horse and cart.'

'I didn't see a horse and cart.'

'No.'

Blood from a stone. So why don't you just shut up, Paris? Because she couldn't, because from the moment she'd first clapped eyes on him—in the flesh, so to speak—two weeks ago, there had been this uncontrollable urge to needle him. 'Horse went lame, did it? Cart broke?' He didn't answer, and she gave a wry smile. He'd already done the Spanish scenes before she'd arrived on the set, then nipped away to whatever else he was currently doing and she'd had the honour of picking him up from the airport, whence he'd flown in his private plane, so that he could complete the mini-epic. Reluctantly, it would appear. 'You don't look like you do on the screen,' she pondered aloud.

'Don't I?'

'No. And this doesn't really seem like the sort of thing you would be involved in.'

'Doesn't it?'

'No. Television series, isn't it?'

'Yes. Sixty minutes of fiction based on fact. Of Isabella following Wellington's army through Spain, rescuing her lover.'

'In an hour?' she asked in amusement. 'So why are *you* doing it? For the money?'

'No. I owed George a favour.'

'What sort of favour?'

Slamming his cup angrily on to the table, he got to his feet. 'God, don't you ever stop asking questions? You sound like a relative of Torquemada!'

'Do I?' she queried softly. 'Because they're questions you can't answer without a script in your hand?'

He opened his mouth, closed it, and then gave her a narrow stare. 'We *are* feeling inadequate, aren't we?' he drawled, not very nicely.

'I beg your pardon?' she asked blankly.

'It has been my experience,' he continued in the same cool tone, 'that such pickiness as you've been displaying usually stems from inadequacy.' With a dismissive little dip of his head, he picked up his wig and started towards the door just as it opened and the funeral director put his head inside.

'We're ready to start,' he explained apologetically.

Oliver nodded, gave her a look of dislike and walked out.

'Damned cheek,' she muttered, 'I don't feel in the least inadequate!'

'Don't,' Henry pleaded. 'Please, don't upset him.'

'More,' she corrected moodily. 'Don't upset him *more.*'

'More,' he agreed as he bent to hunt in one of the cupboards.

'Has a fragile ego, does he?'

'Who, Oliver?' he asked in astonishment. 'Good God, no.'

No? No, possibly not. Possibly it was her own dislike that coloured him grey. Possibly. And she *had* asked for it. Somewhat ashamed of herself, feeling unsettled and irritable, she absently fished a stray tea-leaf from her cup. Unable to leave things alone, needing to know more, she asked, 'Why is he doing George a favour?'

'Because George gave him his first big break.'

'Ah.'

'And this is George's last chance to rescue his reputation. His last two films were, in acting parlance, bummers. Seen any lemons?'

'Oh, Henry.' With a smile that was genuine, more like her old self, she asked gently, 'Cold no better?'

'No,' he said gloomily. 'Worse if anything. I just hope I don't give it to Oliver.'

'Deary me, no; that would be a tragedy.'

He gave her a look of long suffering.

Unrepentant, she peered through the misty window, then grinned as she watched the lovers trudge towards each other through the mud. Henry joined her, then sighed. Sighing seemed to go hand in hand with film-making. 'It wasn't supposed to rain,' he murmured gloomily.

'It wasn't?' she teased. 'You really expected hot sun in November? Anyway, it won't hurt him to rough it for a bit.'

Glancing at her, he reproved gently, 'You're very scathing.'

'Mmm. I don't like actors.' An over-simplification, and not strictly true. She didn't, in fact, really *know* that many actors, so it was totally unfair to lump them all into the same camp as those she *did* know and dislike, but she could hardly tell Henry the real reason for her childish behaviour towards Oliver, even if she fully understood it herself, which she didn't. 'Little prima donnas,' she muttered, 'who constantly suffer for their art.'

'Rather a sweeping statement, and Oliver isn't like that.'

'Isn't he?'

'No.'

'I'll take your word for it.' And maybe he *wasn't* like her rat of a brother-in-law: petulant, childish, a cheat and a liar, who, when he was out of work, borrowed indiscriminately from all and sundry with never a thought to paying it back when he *was* in funds—so why did she keep trying to make herself believe that Oliver was like that? Because of the overpowering awareness that had hit her the moment he'd stepped down from his private plane? Hit her so hard it was really rather frightening? Paris wasn't used to being frightened. And so, in order to get over these damned silly feelings, she *had* to dislike him? Was that it? It didn't need to be *rational*! Anyway, her brother-in-law was like that, she thought moodily and as though it was some sort of justification. And probably the bigger the star, the bigger the ego. Rupert had been like that, too, and *he* was an actor. Rupert, who'd thought she should be grateful for his interest, astonished that she'd minded his affair with another woman, and, in one scathing statement, had mocked her values and wrecked her self-confidence.

Barely aware of Henry, who seemed to be hunting for a lemon alternative, she continued to silently brood on her feelings towards Oliver, and, from there, to her own troubles. Her sister, Athena, and the mess she was now in, all due to her blasted husband, the not-so-famous

Chris Lowery, who was currently swanning round the United States, on *her* savings, in search of meaningful work. She wished Hollywood joy of him. No, she wished they would *employ* him, then he could send for his wife, her sister, who was staying in Paris's flat, because she couldn't afford to stay anywhere else, running *her* into debt, which meant she had to take on any work that was going in order to keep her own head above water. And much as she loved her sister, she was getting just the tiniest bit fed up with the mess she had made in her once immaculate home. And decidedly peeved at the current state of her own finances as she continued to help her sister out.

Still absently watching the confusion outside the trailer, the technicians relaying their miles of snaking cables, lighting experts re-setting their arcs and then hanging on to them like grim death in the fitful wind, she gave a faint smile as she watched Oliver stride to where the roughly made pallet had been artistically arranged in front of the tree-line, and lay down to wait. Paris couldn't see his expression but she imagined it was gritted. Melissa finally finished tippy-toeing through the mud towards him, held her skirts up, and daintily knelt.

'They didn't shout action,' Paris murmured in tones of severe disappointment.

'Oh, gosh, they probably forgot,' Henry muttered, sounding peevish. 'Should I go and tell them, do you think?'

'No!' With an infectious little gurgle of laughter, she turned to look at her companion. He was hunched miserably on the long seat, a picture of dejection. 'Poor Henry,' she commiserated. Reaching above her head, she took the packet of soluble aspirin from the cupboard, dissolved two in a glass of water, and handed it to him.

Boiling up the kettle, she made him fresh tea and placed it on the table beside him.

'Thanks, Paris.' Managing a smile, he asked curiously, 'Why so cynical about it all?'

'Oh, I don't know,' she evaded. 'Is that how I sound?'

'Yes. Don't you like *any* of them?'

'I like you...' she teased.

'But not Oliver?'

She gave a wry smile. 'He rubs me up the wrong way.'

'And that says it all? End of?'

'Mm.' It didn't, of course. She wished it did. He had a gentle smile, did Henry, and, when he wasn't full of cold, probably a kind heart. Paris wasn't sure if her own heart was kind. It *had* been, she thought, but circumstances of late had put too many charges on it, and yet, until certain events had made her view the acting profession with such cynicism, she had treated them with the same amused tolerance she treated everything else, as though they were children in need of guidance. And now *she* was the one in need of guidance. Of the financial variety—and perhaps emotional—because she had not expected that it would be another actor, this particular actor, who would give her such an awareness of self. An awareness that was extraordinarily disturbing, and was being strenuously denied. And would continue to be strenuously denied as long as there was breath in her body. Hence her unusual irritability with Oliver Darke. Adored, fêted, well-paid. Oliver, who did the close-ups, dialogue, *acting*, who got the glory. All normal practice, she believed, so no real need for her disparagement...

With a self-deprecating grin, she shook her head at herself. Your prejudices are showing again, Paris. Yeah. And she surely did have plenty of those. Normally very easy to get along with, easy to talk to, she was friendly

and amusing—but with a stubborn streak a mile wide.
She also tended to make snap judgements about people,
and was never quite sure if the fact that she rarely
changed her mind about them was because she was right,
or stubborn. Although in the case of Oliver Darke it
wasn't stubbornness that kept the prejudice in place, but
fear.

She couldn't actually hear what was being said at the
far end of the field, but she didn't need to be Einstein
to know that something was going very wrong. Again.
Melissa abruptly stood, her back a rigid line of outraged
dignity, Oliver leaned up on one elbow, looked as though
he was saying something exceedingly scathing, and the
director shouted, 'Cut!' There were sundry irritable sighs
and tuttings, and then a peremptory bang on the door
as it was pulled open and one of the technicians put his
head inside.

'Paris, George wants you down with the spectators,'
he told her with almost gleeful mockery. 'Now! Melissa
says they're putting her off.'

'Thank you so much! I've only just got warm,' she
complained.

He smiled. 'Don't shoot the messenger.'

Putting down her cup and half-eaten sandwich,
dragging the collar of her damp raincoat up round her
neck, she hurried out. Here they went again.

The spectators weren't really on his set, she saw, but
an excuse was an excuse, and it was obviously something to focus his temper on. Trudging down the field
towards a straggling group of spectators, mostly children,
she summoned up a smile, asked them to kindly move
back a few paces, explained that they were in camera
shot, which they weren't, and asked if they would remain
very quiet until after the filming. They grinned at her,

obediently moved back, and were instantly silent. How very nice to meet people who did as they were asked without fuss.

Remaining where she was, she watched Oliver and Melissa get themselves back into mood, which, with rain dripping down their necks, was no mean feat, and they made it all so believable, as though they really were desperately in love, desperate to be safe, free. And, having read the script, she knew he was going to die of his wounds. A real tear-jerker.

She watched them embrace, kiss, tried to remain objective—and failed. She felt aroused, felt an awful fluttering in the pit of her stomach, felt hot. Averting her eyes until the love-scene was completed, she sighed along with everybody else when it was decided that it needed to be done again. Melissa flounced round to glare at George—no comfort there, he was adamant—but she seemed to spend an awful lot of time flouncing, did Melissa. Perhaps she was intimidated by having to act with the world's greatest star... Perhaps she just needed a good smack.

The make-up girl dashed up to where Captain Richard Marsh lay wounded. Fresh blood was daubed on his thigh, chest, the side of his face. Melissa's shiny nose was unshined. George examined the scene from all angles and finally nodded.

'OK, let's go.'

A signal was made; Melissa crouched, the clapperboard clapped, and she hesitantly touched Oliver's face, gazed down into pain-filled eyes. Strong arms rose to clasp her tight and mouths met in a sizzling display of passion that made Paris even more aroused than she'd been before. She could almost feel that mouth touching hers, parting, yearning... Turning abruptly away, she stared at the dripping trees, at the spectators, wished she were in Japan, where she'd wanted to be in the first place, and where someone else was in her stead.

'Cut! It's a wrap! Five minutes, everyone, let's get this scene shifted!'

There were sundry thank Gods and an ironic cheer from someone. Melissa hastily stood, was wrapped warmly in a rug by her dresser; Henry hurried off to do the same for Oliver and was waved away.

Glancing up at the lowering sky, and, with the optimistic observation that it looked brighter, George asked Oliver if he wanted to try for the hut scene. Get it all wrapped up in one day.

'If we can. What time is it?'

'Twelve-thirty . . . An hour there, an hour to shoot, if we're lucky. . .' And no one had any tantrums was left unsaid.

Everything was packed up, loaded into the trailers. Paris went to her car—and found Oliver there before her.

CHAPTER TWO

'WELL, don't just stand there with your mouth open, get in. I'll drive,' Oliver said arrogantly.

'I don't want you to drive,' Paris said crossly. 'And why on earth do you want to go in my car? Why not the trailer? And where's Henry?'

'Dosing himself up in the tea-wagon—and I am *not* having him sniffing down my neck for the next half-hour or so. I'd rather have you carping, so just get in, will you?'

Still hovering reluctantly, with absolutely no desire at all to be confined in a car with him, she glanced back at the trailers, wondering whether to beg a lift, when he snapped impatiently, 'I'm not contagious! I have supposed gangrene, not chicken pox! And I want to get these major scenes tidied up today! It's actors who are supposed to be temperamental, not interpreters. I don't need you to *like* me, only direct me to the field,' he concluded more mildly.

Yes, she silently agreed, and if she stood here arguing much longer he would begin to wonder why, wouldn't he? Realise that she usually managed never to be alone with him. 'You aren't supposed to drive round the set. I'll do——'

'Paris!' he gritted. 'Get in the car!'

She got in.

Switching on the engine, he muttered, 'It's bad enough putting up with the restrictions I *have* to put up with! I do not need you to invent more!'

She wasn't inventing them. He *wasn't* supposed to drive round the set. In case of accident. In case filming got delayed, she justified to herself as he pulled out behind the last trailer and up on to the road.

'You should have gone first,' she pointed out five minutes later, when his proximity had become too much, when silence had become too much, 'then you wouldn't have had everyone's mud thrown up on to your windscreen.'

'Which I would have done,' he returned unarguably, 'if a certain someone hadn't shown such reluctance to travel with me.'

Which, of course, probably also made it her fault when a heavily laden farm-truck pulled out in front of them. It laboured slowly up the hill ahead, and when it eventually turned off they'd lost sight of the end camper. He accelerated to catch up, and when they didn't, when the road ahead remained infuriatingly empty, he demanded, 'Where the hell has it gone?'

Not knowing the answer, she kept quiet, just continued to stare through the dirty windscreen, trying to ignore the strong thigh that rested beside her own, the tension that shimmered between them, the awareness, on her side at least, that cramped her muscles, made her edgy. Without any sunlight to filter through the tall trees, it was gloomy, wet, depressing, and, reluctant as she was to admit it, he drove far better than she did, despite losing sight of the trailer.

'We can't have missed the turning, can we?'

'I don't think so, but then, all these roads look the same to me.'

'Well, you've driven the route before! Twice, in fact!'

'True.' So had he. But before, she'd actually been paying attention to the route. This time, she hadn't been.

Neither, obviously, had he. What did he have on *his* mind? Not her, certainly. 'Maybe George knew a short-cut,' she offered without very much hope that it might be true. Reaching for the map that was folded on the dashboard, she opened it, stared at the areas marked with the location of each shot and tried to work out where they might have gone wrong. Or George, in the leading camper, had. 'I don't think it's us,' she finally decided. 'And the only place they could have deviated from the route was about a mile back.'

'They've gone the wrong way?'

'It looks like it.'

'Then perhaps it *is* a short-cut!'

'Perhaps.'

'Well, don't you *know*?' he demanded irritably.

'Obviously not!'

Muttering to himself, he stopped the car, eventually managed to turn it on the narrow road, and began driving back the way they'd come. Paris kept quiet. *She* would have continued on the way she knew, but *she* wasn't driving.

Ten minutes later, and with still no sign of the trailers, she gave him a sideways peek. His face was set and a little nerve jumped in his jaw. His classically sculpted jaw. 'This is silly,' she said softly.

'I *know* that!'

Pulling a face, staring hopefully ahead, she suddenly spotted what she had been looking for. 'Pull over just ahead, in that layby,' she instructed. And, without argument or query, much to her surprise, he did so.

'Now what?'

'We enquire.'

Turning his head to stare at her as though she'd lost all her senses, he raised one eyebrow. The tiny movement spoke volumes.

'That's really very good,' she praised, the regrettable sarcasm back in her voice. 'One slight gesture to imply a wealth of meaning.' Unlatching the door, she added, 'I'll go and see what I can find out.'

'From where?'

She pointed.

'A shed?' he demanded incredulously.

'Yes, Oliver, from a shed.' Not bothering to explain that it was a café, she climbed from the car. Scattering chickens that suddenly appeared from the tree-line in obvious hope of being fed, she crossed the tiny piece of open ground and began to mount the four rickety steps to the porch. Aware that he was following, wishing she felt more able to cope with this disturbing man, she pushed inside and smiled at the elderly woman who turned at their entrance.

She looked incredulous, then mortified, stared round her as though her little enterprise might magically transform itself into a place befitting tourists, stared back at Paris, noticed Oliver, let out a wail and threw her apron over her face.

Equally astounded, Paris turned to look at Oliver, then burst out laughing, her ordinary face transformed into one of gleeful merriment, and it was quite astonishing the difference it made. Having quite forgotten that he was still in his blood-daubed uniform, and that he looked quite desperate, she quickly crossed to the woman, gently touched her shoulder, explained about the film-making; that Oliver was an actor, not really a soldier, and certainly not injured.

The apron was fractionally lowered, and one brown eye hesitantly exposed. '*Sim*?' she queried.

'*Sim,*' Paris reassured.

The apron was restored to its customary place. Glancing rather warily at Oliver, she tried a smile. He smiled back, although Paris didn't think it looked entirely reassuring to this delightful lady who didn't look as though she had ever encountered foreigners first-hand, only heard about them.

'*Café*?' Paris asked hopefully.

'*Dois*?'

'*Sim. Sanduiche*? *Queijo*?'

Still looking rather dubious, the lady nodded, indicated they should sit, and bustled out through a bead curtain at the rear.

'I've ordered coffee and cheese sandwiches, all right?'

'Yes, fine, thanks. Did you ask her about seeing any trailers?'

'No, not yet, she didn't look ready to be interrogated.' Unable to help herself, she grinned.

'No.' Abandoning his stuffiness, he gave a rather wry smile of his own. 'What was the drama all about?'

'Your mortally wounded state,' she explained drily.

Looking momentarily startled, he glanced down at himself, then smiled. 'I'd forgotten I was even wearing it. Did she think...?'

'Yes.' He had a nice smile—if it was genuine. A mouth that promised a lot—and probably delivered more. He also had a nice voice, she decided reluctantly, deep, rich, smooth. Probably had a voice-coach, practised assiduously. Stop it, Paris. With a despairing sigh, she glanced round, chose one of the two obviously handmade tables, and settled herself to wait. Oliver wandered over to look at a flyblown poster tacked to one wall advertising Coca

Cola, and her eyes followed him. His back was straight, good legs shown to great advantage in the tight-fitting buckskins. Powerful thighs. The jacket could have done with being a bit longer...

'1957,' he read, then gave a choke of laughter as he joined her at the table. 'They're not even in the same *decade*!'

'No,' she agreed, 'isn't it great?'

'Great?' he asked in surprise. 'That's a curious statement.'

'Is it? Why?'

'Because most people would——'

'Pity them?' she queried. 'Deride it? Call it quaint, funny, laugh at it? At them?'

'Wouldn't even bother to stop, even if they had known it was a café.' Looking thoughtful, he continued quietly, 'Because they would have assumed it was dirty, ill-kept...' Glancing round him at the well-scrubbed floor, at the rough, but scrupulously clean counter, he looked back at Paris. 'You're a funny girl.'

'Am I?' she asked defensively. 'Why? Because I like the innocence of places like this? Because there are so few places like this left?'

'Untouched by materialism? It looks a grimly hard existence.'

'Yes. But don't...' she began, then stopped.

'Patronise her? Pay over the odds for the coffee? That is what you were going to say, isn't it?'

Yes, it had been. 'Sorry,' she murmured, 'I'm sometimes a bit defensive.'

'Mm,' he agreed drily, 'I had noticed. And despite popular opinion to the contrary,' he offered, somewhat tongue in cheek, 'I'm not just a pretty face.'

'No.' She knew he wasn't, knew there was a very sharp brain behind the façade. Knew he was a law graduate. Henry had told her. And, for the first time since she'd met him, she gave him a genuinely warm smile, a little choke of infectious laughter. 'Life's been a bit fraught of late,' she explained, then turned her smile on the old lady as she returned with their sandwiches and coffee.

She broke into embarrassed speech, and Paris gently touched one gnarled old hand, reassured her.

The woman nodded, smiled back, and returned to her place behind the counter.

'What was that all about?'

Absently stirring her coffee, she explained quietly, 'She was apologising for the cups. Awful, isn't it? That she feels the need to apologise, as though we were better than her, more important, special.'

When he didn't answer, she looked up and surprised a rather odd expression on his face. He also had this trick, if trick it was, of suddenly lifting weighted lids to give a probing look that was very disconcerting. 'What?'

'Nothing,' he denied.

Nothing? It had to be *something*. Was he cross because she'd intimated that he wasn't special? Well, tough. He *wasn't* special.

As though he could read her thoughts, he gave a faint smile, picked up his cup, sipped. 'It's good.'

'Yes, proper coffee. It always is in these outlying places.' Aware that she sounded artificial, but unable to help it, she hurried on. 'The bread and cheese will be, too. No additives, no plastic wrapping, all done the good old-fashioned way.'

'You know Portugal well?'

'The north.'

'And obviously like it.'

'Yes, and the people. Very much.' With another quick smile, she turned towards the old woman, asked if she'd seen any large white trailers pass. She looked confused, thoughtful, then shook her head and broke into speech almost too fast for Paris to follow.

'Nothing has passed this way since early morning,' she explained to Oliver, 'and then only a farm cart, but if we continue on the way we're heading, we'll at least come to the river.'

'Then follow it and hope we come to the field with the hut?'

'Yes.'

'Then we'd better get going, because if George and company have already arrived there,' he said drily, 'and we haven't, then search-parties will be setting out.'

Quickly finishing their snack, Paris paid, because Oliver, still being in costume, had no money on him, smiled at the woman, then thanked her. *'Obrigada. Muito obrigada.'*

'Is that what I say? *Obrigada*?'

'Obrigad-o,' she explained, '"*a*" for me, "*o*" for you. Masculine and feminine.'

With a nod, he too thanked her, and they hurried back to the car. Before, the tension had heightened her awareness. Now that the tension was gone, her awareness took on a different level. A level where she registered everything about him. The way he held his head, his hands on the wheel, the warmth from the strong shoulder that just brushed hers ...

'Which way?'

With a little start, she focused ahead, and realised with some relief that she knew where they were. 'Left, then left again; that should bring us to the field.'

'Should?'

'Will,' she corrected firmly.

'So, if we hadn't stopped...'

'Yes.'

He slanted her a smile that made her feel curiously warm, tried to tell herself it was practised, not meant, then sighed, and when they pulled into the field a few minutes later, a distraught Henry was waiting for them.

'Where the hell have you been?' he demanded as he dragged open Oliver's door.

'On a publicity tour,' he drawled at his most sardonic. 'Always gratifying.'

Leaving Henry with his mouth open, and Paris to give a little grunt of laughter, he strolled off to greet an equally worried-looking George.

So the man could mock himself, Paris thought, as she too climbed from the car. And if he hadn't been an actor, she might even have allowed herself to like him. But he was an actor, a disturbing one, with a media reputation that wasn't entirely savoury, and so it was a road that went nowhere.

'Paris...' Henry complained.

'Mm?' she queried absently as she continued to watch Oliver, then turned to glance at Henry. 'Oh, we got a bit lost,' she explained. 'But he's quite undamaged, and I didn't upset him. Well, no more than usual anyway.' With a distracted smile, she walked down to where it was all happening.

One of the technicians was busily unrolling a piece of wire, and, when it was long enough, he buried it in the grass so that it wouldn't be picked up by the camera, hooked one end on to the pallet, then retreated to the hut, the theory being that as Melissa pulled the injured captain towards his final resting place, the technician would apply equal pressure on the wire—and Melissa wouldn't put her back out. They should have used a travoi, like the Red Indians used. A couple of branches...

'Paris!'

With a little start, she gave the director a weak smile, and moved out of the way. Cameras, that had already been set up while they waited for their star to arrive, were tested, realigned at the gap in the hut wall where two great blocks had been removed, microphones checked, and, when all was ready, George clapped his hands. 'OK everyone, let's get this thing finished.'

Oliver, wig now restored, blood reapplied, lay down on his damp pallet. Melissa bent, lost her footing, and—which Paris found more realistic than anything so far, and was daft enough to say so—swore in a very unladylike way. George shouted, 'Cut,' managing to sound despairing and encouraging all in the same breath—and they began all over again. Melissa dragged her lover into the hut, there was then a brief halt while everyone rearranged themselves, and then they resumed.

Melissa sobbed well, Paris decided, not entirely dispassionately, but not as well as Oliver gave up his struggle with life. Even with all the distractions, the necessary paraphernalia scattered around, the people, Paris felt her throat block, tears start to her eyes as he breathed his last words.

'Dies well, doesn't he?' someone whispered mockingly from beside her.

'Yes,' she agreed thickly, and wanted to sob herself as tension went out of that strong body, as one hand slowly fell to lie at his side, and those beautiful dark brown eyes seemed to actually dim before they became fixed, ever afterwards to stare sightlessly at nothing.

Melissa wailed, crouched protectively over her lover's body, and her broken-hearted sob wrenched at them all.

George's abrupt shout shattered it, made them jump. 'Cut! Brilliant, absolutely brilliant.' Moving forward, rubbing his pudgy hands together, he hugged Melissa, who so far forgot herself as to hug him back. He grabbed Oliver's hand, shook it heartily, and slapped anyone else who happened to be in range. All illusion—and the illusion was now gone.

The group slowly dispersed, the bad temper and frayed nerves replaced by laughter, relaxation—all except Paris, who, for some silly reason, felt betrayed. And he seemed to find it so easy to switch from reality to acting mode. Or wasn't there any real difference? Stand up the real Oliver Darke.

Flattening herself against the doorway to keep out of the way, she continued to watch Oliver. Melissa was whisked away to the comfort of her camper, the crew started to dismantle equipment, begin humping it back to the trailers. Props were gathered up, and everyone began slowly making their way back up the muddy field, then broke into a disorganised rush as the heavens opened and rained on the parade. The few villagers who had come to watch scattered, Paris edged back into the hut, decided no way did she want to be alone with Oliver, and started to retreat.

'The lesser of two evils?' he drawled provocatively.

Halting, she turned to look back. He still sat on his pallet, knees drawn up, elbows resting on them. Without the artificial lighting the hut was dim, shadowy, but still light enough to see the expression in his eyes. An expression that made her feel exceedingly nervous.

'What did you say to Melissa?' he asked quietly. 'I forgot to ask you earlier.'

Oh, hell. 'Melissa?' she queried. 'Why would I say anything to Melissa?'

'Because George asked you to?'

'Oh, yes, well, I didn't say anything very *much*,' she lied. 'But it all went awfully well, I thought, didn't you? Very realistic. Easy, is it? To turn the passion on and off like that?'

'Yes,' he agreed softly. 'It's called acting.'

'At which you are very good.'

'Yes.' Getting lazily to his feet, absently brushing himself off, his eyes never once leaving hers, he persisted, 'What did you say to make her behave like a perfect lady when we all know that *lady* she is not?'

Eyeing him warily, wondering what on earth had happened to his earlier humour, and also knowing that dissension was probably safer, she decided to be honest. Might as well be hung for a sheep as a lamb. 'I told her to be magnanimous.'

'Magnanimous?'

'Yes. That—er—she shouldn't allow you to intimidate her.'

'Because?' he asked, oh, so softly.

'Oh, all right,' she snapped. 'I told her it was the other way about! That you were intimidated by her, hence your bad temper, because she was young, an up-and-coming young star. You were an ageing——'

'Ageing?' he queried silkily.

'Ageing-ish,' she qualified nervously, because this Oliver didn't look at all like the Oliver she had thought she was beginning to know. *This* Oliver looked decidedly dangerous. Edging back towards the doorway, giving herself room, she concluded with rash defiance, 'And you were jealous. Well I had to tell her something! Didn't I? And everyone keeps saying how important it is for George!'

'Mm, then if it was so important for George,' he derided softly, 'why the bad temper towards me? What was that all about? Don't I need to be kept—er—sweet, too?'

'No, yes! It wasn't about anything!'

'No?'

'No!'

'Then why the continual sniping? Bitching about everything I do or say? Life's difficult enough without——'

'*Your* life's difficult?' she exclaimed. '*Yours* is? Well, isn't that a shame? You want to try living *my* life!' Turning on her heel, she took one step to freedom, and was roughly brought back by a strong hand on her arm.

'And just what *is* your life?' he asked as he turned her easily to face him. 'Or is it only that you want some of the action yourself?'

'*What*? No, I do not!'

'No? No yearnings to see your name up in lights? To be clasped to the hero's manly chest?'

'No,' she denied stonily. 'And certainly not to your chest, however manly it might be.'

'Then what? Your name plastered all over the tabloids? "I was Oliver Darke's lover?" Is that it?'

'No, it is not!' she exclaimed furiously. 'You think I want to be like that poor girl you ditched last year?'

His eyes narrowed. '*Poor* girl?' he asked with rather dreadful softness.

Not being naïve enough to think the girl hadn't got *something* out of selling her story to the tabloids, she agreed pithily, 'Not in monetary terms perhaps, but certainly in reputation.'

'Oh, certainly in reputation,' he agreed nastily. 'Deservedly so. And if that really isn't a road you wish to tread, what *do* you want?'

'Nothing, I told you!'

'No? Think I didn't see your expression when we were enacting the last love-scene? And if that wasn't yearning, I don't know what is.'

Opening her mouth to deny it, she closed it again with a snap. She could hardly tell him that was because she'd been aroused, could she?

He gave a cool smile. 'Nothing to say? And your smart remarks just now? They didn't have any meaning, either?'

'No. I was merely curious about the technique,' she returned loftily. 'The ease of... And don't sneer.'

He remained quite still, yet something was different, she didn't quite know what, but suddenly there was a great deal more tension in the air, and his stillness had a subtly menacing quality. 'You don't like me, do you?' he asked quietly.

'No,' she agreed bluntly.

'Why?'

'Does it matter? Or is liking you somehow compulsory? Written into the contract?'

'Don't be bitchy,' he reproved lightly. Drawing her deeper into the shadows, he stared down into her face. 'Because I've ignored you?'

'Don't be absurd.'

'Is it absurd?'

'Yes. And why on earth should it matter to you what I feel?'

'Because you've aroused my curiosity.'

'Rubbish! And even if I had, it was hardly intentional.' Stiffly defiant, her heart beating over-fast, her palms damp, she began to feel suffocated.

'Wasn't it? Not because you wanted to know what it would be like to be kissed by the great Oliver Darke? Act One, Scene One,' he said cynically, and, before she could stop him, he bent his head and kissed her. With a great deal of expertise. Practised expertise. And, even knowing that, it made not a damned bit of difference, because, as she had known, his technique was extraordinary.

CHAPTER THREE

HE KISSED her as he had kissed Melissa, as he had once, presumably, kissed a great many other women. A kiss of pure seduction, searing—utterly impossible to resist. The heat of his body dispersed the damp, dispersed coherent thought. Her mind might insist it was insanity, her body wasn't listening, and when he eventually broke the contact between them she felt mindless, shaken, as though all emotion had been sucked out of her.

'How was the technique?' he asked silkily.

And she couldn't answer, could only stand there, staring at him. Staring into eyes that could make her heart race, at tousled hair plastered down with artificial blood and mud, at a mouth that had proved the promise real.

'Nothing to say?' he taunted.

She shook her head. Shocked, entirely incapable of movement, bereft of feeling, emotion, she choked stupidly, 'You've lost your wig.'

'Have I?' With a mirthless smile, he turned and walked out.

Practised emotions, practised expressions. Who was the real Oliver Darke? Or wasn't there one? Was it impossible to separate the screen image from the man? A man who created illusion? And she had asked for everything she got. She'd been goading him, needling him ever since they met. Why? For this one reason? Because she had for once in her life wanted to feel what her sister often boasted about? The glamour of the acting profession, the excitement, the famous stars? The warmth, the laughter, the passion? No! Dear God, no! Surely she wasn't so shallow? She had her own life, her own friends, her own career; surely, surely she hadn't, even in the deepest recesses of her mind, wanted to be like Athena. Or how Athena had become since being married to Chris. Once she had been loving, sometimes selfish, but kind, happy. Now she was mercurial, temperamental, thoughtless and childish—pretty. Paris was twenty-nine years old! Not a child! And she had *never* wanted the supposed glamour that her sister so loved. Never. If she had, she would have stayed with Rupert, no matter what it might have cost her!

Disturbed, still dazed, she wandered outside, and, as though the elements wanted to show everyone how it was really done, like a silver screen, a soft, wet curtain of light, the rain moved away, up into the hills. A patch of blue appeared, a weak sun to throw a gentle glow over the little village that was divided by the small, winding road that led, eventually, to Oporto. She didn't know how long she stood there, just staring ahead—ten minutes, half an hour—but when she turned she saw that only one trailer remained. The tea-wagon. With a little shudder, head down, she trudged up the field towards her car.

'Get a move on, Paris,' Henry shouted from the driver's cab of the long camper. 'I'll follow you out.'

Lifting one hand in acknowledgement, not even pausing to wonder what on earth he was doing driving the tea-wagon, she hurried to her car, climbed into its comforting anonymity and drove out on to the road that would take them back to Espinho and the comfort of the hotel for the night. A different road to the one they had come in on, the road that ran beside the swollen river. Her mind more on what had happened in the hut than what was going on around her, she was almost past the little farmstead before she actually registered what she had seen. Slamming on her brakes, she stared with horror at the flood water that was slowly consuming the land around it, at the old lady who was struggling to rescue her possessions. Shoving the gear lever into neutral and dragging on the brake, she got out, hurried back, shouted across to her.

'Paris!' Henry yelled. 'What on earth are you doing? Don't leave your car there!'

Swinging around, she shouted, 'We can't leave her! She needs help!'

'*We* can't leave her?' he queried sarcastically.

'All right! *I* can't leave her!'

She heard him mutter something rude and thereafter ignored him. Hurrying down the incline, wading into the rapidly rising water where the river had broken its banks, she grabbed the pile of bedding the old lady was holding, turned, and saw Oliver wading towards her. Shocked, because she hadn't known he was with Henry, reluctant to face him, she avoided eye-contact and thrust the bundle in his general direction. 'Shove everything in the trailer,' she ordered peremptorily. Not waiting to see if he did what he was told, she hurried back to the open door of the farmhouse.

Slipping and sliding in the mud, her boots clogged, her raincoat flapping, she saw the chickens for the first time, shouted a query to the old woman, and then began trying to round them up. And, because she was the only one of them who spoke the language, shouts kept going up for her as she dashed back and forth, interpreting and issuing her own orders.

Grabbing a chair that had been piled on top of an old bench, she turned and nearly damaged Oliver. Nerves still stretched tight, not really knowing what to do or say, she snapped stupidly, 'There are still chickens loose!'

'I dare say there are, but if you bothered to actually look at me instead of round me, through me, or whatever else it is you're doing, you would see that I already have my hands full!'

With a little sniff, she trudged past him with her chair and pushed it into the open door of the trailer. Oliver leaned past her and dumped his own armful beside it. 'And where, might I ask, are we to take all this stuff when we've loaded it?'

'The next village,' she muttered, still without actually looking at him. 'She has friends there.'

'Right.' Turning on his heel, he stalked back to the farmhouse just as Henry arrived trying to juggle a blanket-wrapped bundle, two cooking-pots and a large pot-plant. It was beginning to get dark.

'Oliver!' Henry shouted after him. 'For goodness' sake don't run like that! If you fall and break a leg... And be careful of your face!'

Oliver ignored him.

'Idiot,' he muttered. Swinging back to Paris, he castigated, 'Why the hell can't she put some damned lights on? I can't see what the hell I'm doing!'

'What damned lights?' she snapped. 'They don't have any.'

He threw her a look of astonishment. 'Good God.'

'Quite. Unless you'd like a candle, of course!' Relieving him of the plant, she wedged it between the chair and the bundle Oliver had rescued.

'And why is she here on her own? An old lady like that! It's scandalous!'

'She isn't normally on her own. Her son and daughter-in-law are in Espinho. Not due back until tomorrow.'

'Oh.'

'Yes,' she agreed. 'Oh.'

'And you've become very bossy!' he complained as he turned to wade back to get something else.

She hadn't *become* bossy! She was *always* bossy! No, she wasn't. Normally she was unobtrusive, or so she thought, faded into the wallpaper. Pitched in, helped out... With a long sigh, she trudged off to look for livestock.

'Paris!'

Turning, seeing Oliver trying to restrain the owner, she grabbed a passing chicken and shouted, 'What?'

'She wants to take her bloody bed!'

'Then help her!'

'Don't be daft! It won't go through the door!'

'Then dismantle it!'

'We don't have time! For God's sake, Paris, just look where the river is!'

'I'm looking!' Releasing the chicken, she hurried over, then explained in short, pithy, terms, 'It's probably her most prized possession! She's no doubt scrimped and saved for years to buy it! She can't just claim on the bloody insurance if it gets lost! They don't *have* insurance! What they lose stays lost! They can't afford to replace things like we can! Now move!' Speaking quickly to the old lady, reassuring her, she asked her to explain how it dismantled. A wide, relieved smile was thrown at her and she practically shoved Oliver in through her front door. Serve him right. Knock some of the pomposity out of him! Water was just touching her calves.

By the time they'd finished, the precious bed safely stowed, the old lady having a final check round, Paris leaned against the side of the camper, Henry beside her.

'Thanks,' she said quietly.

He gave her a tired smile. 'Not your place to thank me. I might have been a bit slow off the mark, but not reluctant, Paris.' Turning to stare at the rapidly spreading water, he mused, 'Seems a funny place to build your home. Right on the riverbank.'

'Yes,' she agreed inadequately.

With another tired smile, he patted her shoulder and levered himself upright. 'I'd better go and look for the lost chicken. Can't have the egg ratio down, can we?'

'No,' she smiled.

Ambling off, he left Paris to her contemplation of the scene before her. A scene that now included Oliver's back. He was perched on the wall in front of her, examining one hand. The jeans he'd changed into were soaked to above the knee, his grey sweatshirt wet and muddy, the blond hair tousled. A strong back, the shoulders wide, a nice place to rest a weary head. With a grim little smile she wrenched her gaze away to absently watch a mangy-looking dog walk slowly down the road towards them. It looked as dejected as she felt. And yet, at the end of the day, it was only fantasy, wasn't it? This undefined yearning, this need. So why, if she knew that, didn't it go away? Why couldn't she laugh about it? Because it *was* funny, wasn't it? Lusting after one of the most well-known actors of the day. No, she thought with a long sigh, it wasn't funny at all. She'd waited all her adult life to feel the way she had felt when he'd kissed her—and it had to be a film star. A hero of the silver-screen. She could still almost feel the touch of his mouth on hers, the feel of his hands on her shoulders, and she shivered.

The dog reached her, sat, looked hopeful, scratched.

'Not more bloody livestock,' Oliver complained tartly. 'Damned thing's probably got fleas!'

Flinging her head up in a reflex action, she stared at him. He'd swivelled round on the wall and was now facing her. Hastily averting her gaze, she agreed tonelessly. 'Probably.'

He sighed, the dog gave him a look that could only be described as dismissive, got to his feet and wandered off. 'Probably seen one of my films,' he observed mournfully.

'Yes.' She tried for a smile, and couldn't quite manage it. She knew he was watching her, could feel his eyes on her, and refused to look up.

'Not amused, I see.'

'No.'

His sigh was deeper, longer. 'It was only a damned kiss!'

'Yes.' Only a damned kiss.

'You want me to apologise, is that it?'

'No,' she denied woodenly.

'Then stop bloody sulking!'

Looking up to glare at him, she insisted, 'I am not sulking! And I did not *ask* for it,' she retorted in remembered anger. 'Did not want *anything*. And I don't know why you thought I *did*!'

'Because women do,' he said, somewhat bleakly. 'Why should you be any different?'

'Because I *am*! It was practically an assau——'

'Oliver!' Henry roared as he hurried up. 'What the hell do you think you're doing? Get off that damp wall! You'll catch your death!'

'Don't be ridiculous,' he snapped. 'You don't catch your death from sitting on a damp wall!'

'Piles, then.'

'Oh, charming! That'll look well in the world's Press, won't it? Famous actor goes down with piles!' Getting to his feet, he stormed off.

'What's up with him?' Henry demanded in astonishment. 'What have you been saying?'

'Nothing, and do put that chicken down! You look extremely silly!'

Glancing down at the chicken, he dropped it into the makeshift pen as though it were a hot potato. 'And that's another thing! What are we supposed to do with them? They can't go in the camper!'

'Why not?' she asked irritably.

'Why not? Why not? Use your brain, Paris! We'll be knee-deep in chicken sh...manure,' he hastily substituted, 'before we've gone half a mile!'

With a reluctant grunt of laughter, she stared at him helplessly. 'Oh, Henry, what a day.' Straightening, she went to have a word with the old lady. Moments later, both men came to see what the argument was about.

'She wants to put them in the boot of the car!' Paris exclaimed.

'Oh, what a good idea,' Oliver drawled approvingly.

Rounding on him, she shouted, 'Don't be so stupid! What the hell are the hire company going to say when they see the boot covered in chicken...mess?'

'They won't look,' he said impatiently, 'and even if they do, just put on your innocent expression and tell them it must have been like that when you hired it! If you can boss us all about, I'm sure as hell sure you can do the same with a car-hire company! They're not *nearly*

so important! Now, can we for God's sake get this show
on the road?' Turning away, he went to grab a chicken.

Henry snorted, got glared at, and meekly went to help.

Wrenching open the boot, determined not to see the
funny side of it, Paris muttered, 'And if they die of suf-
focation, or carbon monoxide poisoning, *I'm* not paying
the compensation!' Staring at the men's innocent
expressions, and the old lady's blank one, she gave a
reluctant smile. They looked like the Three Stooges. 'Oh,'
she exclaimed, 'just get on with it. And find me a
newspaper!'

Henry meekly found her an old dog-eared script which
she tore apart and carefully lined the boot with, then
oversaw the placing of the chickens.

'You never know,' Oliver whispered close to her ear,
'they might lay you some nice little eggies for your tea.'

'Shut up, Oliver! Just shut up!' Swinging round to
glare, she found him much too close, and took a hasty
step backwards.

'And I don't know why you're glaring, *I'm* the one
who's been abused. Shouted at, derided, my fragile ego
bruised. You've dragged me into a wooden hut, forced
your opinions down my throat, thrust me into misad-
venture. I've been thoroughly soaked, had chickens
shoved at me—it isn't at all what I'm used to, you know.
I'm a film star.'

She tried to maintain her glare, felt her lips twitch,
and looked quickly down, reached out to close the boot.

'And just as a point of interest,' he asked lazily, 'has
anyone ever tried to strangle you?'

She nodded, a little glint of mischief in her eyes.
'Frequently.'

'And have obviously never succeeded.'

'No.' Giving him a sideways look, she murmured irrepressibly, 'I'm fast on my feet.'

Laughter flickered in the back of his eyes, warmth softened his face, then he chuckled and turned away to hold the passenger door open for the old lady.

Climbing quickly behind the wheel, she caught a glimpse of herself in the rear-view mirror. She was grinning like an idiot. Fool, Paris. You don't like actors, remember?

Turning to automatically check that the road was clear, she caught Oliver's eye as he climbed up into the trailer beside Henry, and gave a helpless laugh, because it *was* so absurd. And if his adored fans could see him now, they would adore him even more. Sobering, she thrust the car into drive, smiled reassuringly at her passenger, and set off on the two-mile journey to the next village.

While the old lady went to explain to her friends, Paris went to check on the chickens, and the men to unload the belongings. Half an hour later, their mission of mercy accomplished, they were ready to resume their journey, and all that remained was for Paris to give a message to the old lady's son on their way through Espinho.

'I'll come with you,' Oliver declared unexpectedly. 'In fact, I'll do the driving; we can't have our intrepid heroine drive alone in the dark.'

Giving him a look of astonishment, but too tired to argue, she merely nodded and climbed into the passenger seat. She felt wet, uncomfortable, weary, and being squashed up with Oliver in the narrow confines of the car seemed—nice. They waved to the abandoned Henry and set off. They found the address the old lady had given her without too much trouble, and, when Paris was back in the car, clutching a little bottle of something or other that the son had pressed on her, they drove back across the railway line and along to the hotel. The hotel that had been closed for refurbishment, the hotel that had opened up the dining-room with reduced staff, allowed them to use one floor, because it had been an offer too good to refuse. Not everyone was prejudiced against film crews.

The trailers were all lined up on the beach ready to be driven to Santander and the ferry to England if George gave the word after he'd reviewed the day's rushes; flights would be booked, suitcases packed, and she would go back to her troubled life, put Oliver behind her, and, hopefully, her muddled feelings. And it all seemed a rather flat end to it all. Undoing her seatbelt, she gave a soft little sigh and reached for the door-catch.

'I'll apologise if you will,' he said softly.

Surprised, she swung round to face him. There was a faint humorous quirk to his sensuous mouth, laughter deep in his eyes. Fighting off the urge to retreat, get out now, escape, she stared rather worriedly at him, then sighed and shook her head. 'No,' she denied quietly, 'I think it's the other way about.'

'Only think?' he teased.

'No,' she admitted with a comically wry little grimace, 'know. I've been behaving like an idiot, deliberately obstructive.'

'Why?' he asked gently.

'Oh,' she prevaricated, 'I don't know.' And it was absurd, but she felt so embarrassed, awkward, gauche, as though she had never been intimate with a man before, never been kissed, never mind one that had not been meant.

'You put a label on me, didn't you?' he asked, his voice still gentle, understanding. 'And then never bothered to look past the glue.'

'No... Yes,' she admitted reluctantly. She hadn't *wanted* to look past the glue. She'd deliberately made him two-dimensional, and of course he wasn't. She had also thought herself secure enough, capable enough, to cope with most things that life threw at her—until the disturbing reaction to his appearance in her life, to the way he'd kissed Melissa, and then herself. And it was all so silly, this yearning after a film star. Utterly absurd to give credence to the feelings he generated in her— generated in millions of other women, too, no doubt. So why on earth couldn't she separate fact from fiction? She wasn't a fool—or hadn't been, until now.

'Not going to tell me why?'

She shook her head.

'All right,' he agreed gently. 'Change of subject?'

Still wary, but grateful that he seemed to understand, she nodded. 'Please.' And then decided that she really did need to know why, clarify... 'Do women behave like that? Expect—want—pursue you for what they can get?'

'Yes,' he said simply.

'That woman in the paper?'

'Yes.'

'Oh. But *I* wasn't... I mean, I didn't...' Cross with herself for being so inarticulate, she added firmly, 'That wasn't what I was doing!'

'Wasn't it?'

'No.'

'Then what were you doing?' he teased, then laughed when she looked confused. 'OK, unfair question.' Settling himself, the faint smile still in the back of his eyes, he commented, 'You were pretty quick off the mark just now. I didn't even notice the farm, let alone the flooding.'

And that was it? She didn't even know if he believed her. Rather mortifying to think that he might not. But if she pursued it, it would give it an importance it mustn't have.

'Done that sort of thing before, have you?' he continued easily. 'Rescuing elderly ladies?'

'No, although I dare say I over-reacted, as usual,' she murmured with a wry little smile of her own. 'I imagine she would have coped perfectly well without my intervention.'

'Not with the bed she wouldn't!'

Diverted, she gave a weak chuckle. 'Poor you.'

'Not poor me,' he corrected. 'It might have taught me something about values. Taught us all. And we think ourselves deprived if the television goes on the blink. It's a whole different world, Paris, isn't it?'

'Yes. And yet I don't imagine she feels herself hard done by. This is her life, the way she's always lived.'

'A piece of land, a loving family, enough to eat? A simple life—or so it looks to others. I imagine it's unbelievably hard.'

'Yes, and yet I think these country people are the most cheerful I've ever met. Friendly, kind, humorous.'

'Generous? What's in the bottle?'

'I don't know—some sort of local brew, I imagine.' Unscrewing the top, she sniffed, then experimentally sipped. 'Wine?' she guessed.

Taking the bottle, he touched the neck with his tongue. 'Brandy?'

'Typhoid?' she quipped.

He choked, then laughed. 'Well, if it is, don't for God's sake tell Henry!'

'I won't. Whatever else I may be, I'm not a snitch.'

'No, I never supposed you were.'

Turning her face towards him, she sighed, and managed a smile. He smiled back, and her silly heart turned over. Even looking like a sludge-bucket, he was devastating. Mud across one cheekbone, his hair damp, dishevelled, hands grimy, and now that he was being friendly, self-mocking, he was extraordinarily difficult to dislike. And yet, oddly enough, whenever she'd seen him at the cinema, she'd liked him as an actor, admired him, but she hadn't felt this ridiculous awareness. It wasn't adoration because he was famous; it wasn't even a form of excitement, awe; it was something more, something she didn't entirely understand.

'Why the sigh?' he asked kindly. 'Tired?'

'Mmm,' she agreed, 'a bit.' It was an acceptable excuse, and partially true. Wrenching her gaze from his, she stared at the lighted hotel in front of them, felt tension begin to filter back.

'You work for George's brother, don't you?'

'Yes, he runs the translation agency.'

'Are they alike?'

'Only in looks. George shouts, William wheedles.'

'And wheedled you out here? When you didn't want to come?' he tacked on softly.

Giving him a little glance from the corner of her eyes, she grinned. 'That obvious, huh? I wanted to go to Japan. Should have been going to Japan.'

'You don't like Portugal?'

'I love Portugal, and normally would have been delighted to come. I like the language, the people, the scenery, especially here on the green coast. It's truly lovely when the weather's good, but...'

'You wanted to practise your Japanese?'

'Mmm, and see the country. I've never been there, you see.'

'A good enough reason, probably better weather, too.'

'Yes, but George was calling in favours, wasn't he?'

'Yes,' he agreed, 'and his brother, William, was obviously no more proof against his persuasions than the rest of us—because we all knew,' he added quietly, 'that, unlike Melissa, he isn't flavour of the month. That his last two films were flops...'

'And if he doesn't succeed with this one?'

He made a cutting motion at his throat. 'It's a sad fact of life that when you're down, nothing goes right. Past glories, achievements, count for nothing.'

'And there's nothing worse than being a has-been,' she stated softly. Better never to have achieved at all, Paris sometimes thought. People could be very scathing about failure. About success, too. You could fight, achieve, be fêted, adored, and when you were up there, those same people who had put you there tried to knock you down, and when they succeeded, as they so often did, they were merciless in their scorn. 'That's why this production is so important to him?'

'Mmm, and if the television company like it, as please God they will, he has the option to do six more.'

'They'll like it,' she encouraged positively. And they probably would, because Oliver Darke was in it—and he was a very good actor.

'I hope so, for George's sake. What made you become an interpreter?' he asked curiously.

With one of her comical little grimaces, she explained drily, 'It was the only thing I was good at.'

'School?'

'Useless.'

'Fibber.' He grinned. 'You couldn't have been that useless if you manage to translate goodness knows how many languages.'

'Maybe,' she shrugged. 'And you? Why did you become an actor?'

'The same.'

'The only thing you were good at?'

'Mm.'

'Liar,' she reproved softly. 'Henry told me you have a law degree, that you're one of those wretched people who excel at whatever they turn their hand to.'

'Henry seems to have said altogether far too much. Which isn't like him at all,' he mused softly to himself.

'And if he could see you now, he would tell *you* to go and get out of those wet clothes. You're a very valuable property.'

'And you aren't? To anyone?'

With another little shrug, she admitted, 'Not at the moment.'

'No parents?'

'No. They died a long time ago. Ten years,' she said softly. 'They were quite elderly when they had us. A late family. When Mum died, I don't think Dad wanted to go on without her; he died barely a year later.'

'Wretched for you.'

'Yes.'

'Us?' he queried gently.

'I have a sister.'

'No lover? Man in your life?'

She shook her head. Not wanting to talk about herself any more, her life, she asked, 'Why does Henry always wear black?'

He grinned. 'Someone once told him he looked like a pall-bearer. It amused him, so he now dresses accordingly.'

Rather a glib explanation, but probably true. 'We'd better go in,' she urged as he absently peeled his wet jeans away from his thigh. 'Hot properties mustn't be allowed to get chilled, although, now that filming's finished, I imagine you'll be off to warmer climes, or something,' she murmured, her prejudices not entirely dissipated.

'I wish!' he exclaimed. 'I have another film I need to finish; the studio reluctantly released me for a couple of weeks in order to help George out.'

'Oh.'

He smiled. A smile that was teasingly malicious. 'You thought I was playing the big star, didn't you? Being magnanimous. Nipping in for the glory bits, get the recognition. No, no, don't deny it, and don't explain; your real reason for the dislike might be worse. Think of my ego!'

With an acknowledging smile, she removed the bottle from his hand, carefully screwed the top back on, and reached for the door-handle.

'Retreating in good order, Paris?'

And something in his tone made her nervous. Nothing readily identifiable, just—something. 'Mmm,' she murmured without turning. And, if George was happy with the day's takes, tomorrow he would be gone, and then maybe, just maybe, she could get her life back together. And, deciding that words, any words, might dispel the nervousness she was feeling, she looked back to ask, 'Were you really getting into the mood when I disturbed you in the hut this morning?'

'Of course. I was practising a sightless gaze,' he said straight-faced, just the tiniest twitch to his lips to give the game away. 'And in the caravan I was trying to get into the mood of the part!'

'Oh. Sorry,' she apologised belatedly.

Moving into a more comfortable position, his eyes on her downcast face, he queried gently, 'Don't like actors, Paris? Not allowed, you know. We thrive on adoration. And, instead of chatting here to you, I should be busily giving everyone in the town my autograph...'

'I don't think they know who you are,' she said solemnly, and he grinned, the grin that set a million hearts swooning. Or was it?

'Still determined to put me down?' he queried humorously.

'Sorry,' she apologised again, quite unrepentantly.

He touched an admonishing finger to her cheek. 'It's just a job, you know. Like any other.'

'Sure.' With a little shiver, she moved her head away, and his smile died; the light of laughter in his eyes flickered and went out.

Her own eyes suddenly wide, wary, her heartbeat accelerating uncomfortably, she warned huskily, 'Oliver...'

Removing his elbow from the back of the seat, his movement slow, pre-ordained almost, he slid his hand to her nape, urged her forward and, ignoring her resistance, gently touched his mouth to hers, until the breath jerked in her throat. 'I can't get it out of my mind,' he murmured against her lips, 'the feel of it, the warmth.' And then proceeded to increase that warmth, part her mouth with eager insistence, gather her close, and the kiss deepened, became urgent.

'No,' she groaned. Trying to push him away in the narrow confines of the car, her palm slid from his damp shoulder to his warm neck, felt the little pulse throbbing there, and she shuddered. 'Oliver, you said—didn't believe...'

'Shh,' he murmured throatily as he continued to taste the sweetness of her, sending long shivers down her back, curling painful heat into her stomach, and, as his other hand splayed across her spine, urging her yet closer, she felt her resistance slipping and fought to retain her sanity. Pure seduction, her mind whispered hazily, but the excitement of it, the hunger of it, was crumbling her defences.

The throbbing pulse in his neck seemed to echo her own heartbeat, the feel of his hair tickling her fingertips, a sensuous delight, and, just as she felt her body begin to melt into his, he broke free. 'Not wise,' he said, and his voice was thick, husky, his breathing ever so slightly uneven. 'Pure vanity, because I wanted you to know...' With a little shake of his head, a smile that was almost rueful, he added softly, 'From me. The person, not the actor. My own technique, because you sometimes have trouble differentiating between the two, don't you?' His arms slowly leaving her, his beautiful brown eyes still intent, serious, he finally found a warmer smile, and Paris did not know if it was real or false. 'Although I'm mighty glad to see that it *also* leaves you speechless.' Turning away, he quickly removed the keys from the ignition and reached for his own handle.

'Oliver,' she managed huskily, and then didn't know what to say, only knew that she needed to make it clear that she wasn't a player.

He turned, searched her face, then smiled gently. 'No discussion, no analysis, let's just ride the rainbow, hmm? Come on, let's get out of these wet clothes.'

Ride the rainbow? What did that mean? Wait and see if there was gold at the end? Or only an empty crock? Still staring blankly after him, mesmerised almost, worried and bewildered, she got out and walked rather dazedly into Reception. Speechless? Oh, yes. And confused, and aching. And had that been just another job?

Because he thought that was what she'd expected? Wanted? And if you were pretty, you *could* expect things like that. But she wasn't pretty—and she didn't. So why had he done it? From *me*, he'd said, the man, not the actor, but in her experience, limited admittedly, there seemed little difference between the two. Acting seemed to take over your life to the exclusion of all else. It had affected Chris that way, made her sister hard. And Rupert, whom she'd once loved—no, not loved; if she had, she would probably have stayed with him, even though he'd changed so much. Celebrity status, the pursuit of stardom, had altered his values. Everything had to suffer for his art, including herself. But she hadn't wanted to suffer, had refused to do so, because she had wanted more from life than to be someone's ego-booster, someone's prompt. A shoulder when they were down, ignored when they were up. No, she wanted more from life than that. Wanted to be a person in her own right, not an extension of someone else's. And if Rupert's kisses had made her feel a tenth of what Oliver's had done... And Oliver hadn't been entirely unaffected, had he? His voice had been thicker... and he'd said...

Don't be dumb, Paris. With a long, troubled sigh, she looked up, focused ahead, and felt a clawing pain inside. Oliver was standing at the desk, Melissa beside him, and, even as she watched, the young actress reached up, one small hand on Oliver's shoulder, and pressed a kiss to his mouth. Oliver laughed, hooked her against him, kissing her back.

She felt diminished, stupid, because she had thought he didn't even like the young starlet... With a twisted smile, because she *knew* that actors didn't have to like someone to go around kissing them, she quickly averted her eyes, managed a vague smile for one of the receptionists, then grimaced ruefully at her look of horror for the state she was in, and thankfully handed over her filthy mac and boots to be cleaned. Collecting her key, and the letter that had been tucked in her pigeonhole, she walked across the foyer, and it wasn't until she was halfway up the stairs that she fully understood why he had kissed her, what he had been trying to achieve. What Rupert had been so good at achieving. He had charmed away her sulks, left another adoring fan in his magnificent wake. And that *was*, probably, what he had been doing. Actors acted all the time, didn't they? *Didn't* they? And if she hadn't seen him with Melissa, might she not have been tempted into believing that his kisses had been meant?

CHAPTER FOUR

'PARIS!'

Halting, she stiffened and slowly turned to see Oliver bounding up the stairs behind her.

'I forgot to ask you something.'

'What? Did I mind being practised on?'

'Sorry?' he queried in confusion.

She gave him an arctic smile. 'And, although I am very well aware that the acting profession *acts*, I do not like being used.'

Turning away, she continued her ascent. She could almost hear him thinking about it, what she had said, and then his footsteps sounded again and she was brought to an abrupt halt. He moved in front of her, blocked her progress, stared at her, and said quietly, 'Would you like to run that by me again?'

'No.'

Leaning his elbow on the banister, he propped his chin in his hand and continued to watch her. 'Are we referring to the kiss?'

She kept her expression blank, stared back.

'Practise? I don't *need* to practise!' he murmured with dry humour.

'How very nice for you.'

'You saw me kiss Melissa.' A statement, not a question.

And when she remained silent, the same quizzical expression on his face, he asked softly, 'Jealous?'

57

Her mouth tight, she tried to step past him, only to be thwarted by him stepping in front of her. 'Let me past.'

'No.' And odd little smile playing about his mouth, he murmured, 'Some time in the future, Melissa and I might have to work together again. The kiss was—expedient.' Hooking her against him, much as he had hooked the starlet, he kissed her very quickly, very impersonally, on the mouth. 'Like that. Not,' he added even more softly, 'like this.' He bent again, parted her surprised mouth with gentle insistence, touched his tongue fleetingly to hers, and stepped back. With a slightly mocking smile, he turned away, ran lightly up the remaining stairs and disappeared along the corridor that led to his room.

Feeling stupid, her fingers unconsciously touching her mouth, suddenly realising that she would be in full view of anyone above or below, she scurried up to her own room, thankfully closed the door. And she still didn't know why he had kissed her! Because he'd felt like it, presumably! Sinking down on to the edge of the bed, aware she was still clutching the note the receptionist had given her, and assuming it was from George with the next day's schedule, she absently opened it, and was astonished to see that it was a telephone message from her sister. Frowning, she slowly reread it. Why on earth would Athena want to come out here? A stop-over, the note said. Stop over to where? Oh, heavens, surely not more trouble. And she didn't *want* Athena out here. That sounded awful, and, although she loved her, was generally pleased to see her, she liked to keep her own working life separate.

Lying back on the bed, the note still in her hand, she stared up at the ceiling. Jealousy, Paris? No, she didn't honestly think it was that, it was just that Athena was so disruptive! And she'd come here to temporarily escape her troubles, not bring them with her. Athena tended to deal in half-truths, innuendo—teasing, she called it, but it was a teasing that was often misconstrued. Paris wasn't jealous of her sister's beauty, her lifestyle, yet Athena always managed to make people believe that she was, and she had learnt over the years that denial only made things worse. 'Teasing' was a very difficult weapon to counter, and, although she was secure enough in her own abilities not to be hurt, she did get a bit *peeved* by it. And she had never really understood why 'glamour' was so envied by others. *She* didn't envy it. Oh, well, she thought, trying to be philosophical, Athena would no doubt reveal all when she arrived in the morning for her 'stop-over'.

Getting to her feet, she went to shower and wash and dry her hair. Wrestling with the wardrobe door, which kept getting stuck, owing no doubt to the fact that the varnish had been half stripped from it during the refurbishment process which the film crew had interrupted, she dressed in a navy wool dress, draped a silk scarf at her throat, stared thoughtfully at herself in the long mirror, and removed it. Gilding the lily, she thought with a rather sad smile—and no amount of gilding would make this lily look anything but ordinary. Elegant, but ordinary.

Pushing her feet into high-heeled navy shoes, collecting her bag, desperately trying to put into perspective the feel of a warm mouth parting her own— because it had been a teasing kiss, she told herself firmly, a kiss that meant nothing, because kisses were an actor's stock in trade—she forced herself to consider Athena's forthcoming visit, anticipate the problems so that she might deal with them. And if Melissa's kiss *had* been expedient, why had he said their own hadn't been wise? Because she might get ideas? Oh, will you stop *thinking* about it! Wrenching open the bedroom door, she hurried downstairs.

Most of the crew were already in the restaurant when she pushed inside, and they smiled or waved, inviting her to sit with them, but she elected to sit at her little table in the corner where she could watch the sea crashing against the rocky promontory. And have a good long think.

'Don't forget the party in the bar this evening,' George called across. 'Last night of filming; it's traditional!'

'Last night?' she queried. 'We've finished?'

He nodded, smiled.

Oh. And that meant—she wouldn't see him any more, wouldn't see Oliver. So the kiss had probably been in the nature of a parting gift—and he'd mentioned rainbows, because they were ephemeral, never meant to last. Feeling a little bit lost, she stared from the window. Wished, in a way, that it were already tomorrow, that all this were behind her, and then she saw him come in, saw him glance round, and she stiffened, prayed he wouldn't come over to sit with her, then breathed a sigh of relief when he sat with George. It didn't stop her discreetly watching him, though, and it was becoming obsessive, wasn't it, this need to keep watching him? Trying to analyse his behaviour? Her own? The ridiculous awareness that made her tremble. He was freshly showered and shaved, dressed in a dark cream open-necked knit shirt and dark trousers, and he looked vibrant, alive, despite the sleepy eyes, his skin glowing with health. A star, entirely out of her reach, as all stars were. Unless you had a spaceship, which she didn't. Nor the wherewithal to buy one. She would have one drink in the bar, she decided, and then go to bed, think about herself for a change. Sounded so easy when it was said.

Dawdling over her meal, she watched them leave one by one, heard them go into the bar. Coffee-cup nursed in her palms, she gave a faint sigh, and tomorrow she would find out for sure what sort of mess Athena had left her in this time. And, if Athena came early enough, before the crew left, pin a smile on her face as she watched her sister flirt with them. And she would. Flirting came as naturally as breathing to her sister. Don't get peevish, Paris, it's not nice.

'You're looking very pensive,' Oliver observed.

With a little start, she looked up, felt colour wash into her face and looked hastily away. 'Oh, hello, I didn't see you,' she murmured with an attempt at offhandedness which didn't quite come off.

'No,' he agreed with a faint smile. 'It makes a nice change. Or it would have made a nice change,' he qualified with a grin, 'if I hadn't *wanted* you to see me.' Grabbing a chair from the table behind him, he turned it round and sat opposite her.

'I haven't the faintest idea what you're talking about!' she muttered crossly.

'I know you haven't, that's what makes it so nice. Famous star?' he prompted teasingly. 'Never mind,' he comforted when she continued to look lost. 'Just one of those statements that don't bear explaining.' Propping his elbows on the table, chin in his palms, he grinned. 'Due to—er—being distracted earlier, I didn't get the chance to ask you.' Adopting his best little-boy-lost look, he added, 'I need a favour.'

'Favour?' she asked cautiously. 'What sort of favour?'

'An interpreting favour.' Reaching across the table, he picked up one of her hands and gave her a winning smile. 'There's someone I need to talk with, a business venture... Have you ever been in that restaurant down the road? The one with the green awning?'

'Yes,' she agreed, still cautiously, and, unbearably conscious of the feel of his warm fingers holding hers, she carefully withdrew her hand, made the excuse of needing to stir her coffee.

His own hand, left with nothing to do, idly picked up the salt pot, revolved it in his long fingers. 'The owner has a yearning to open a restaurant in London. I *have* a restaurant in London, which isn't doing terribly well,' he added ruefully. 'And so, if we can come to a satisfactory agreement... Unfortunately, his English isn't very good, and, as you know, my Portuguese is non-existent...'

'And you both need to be sure of exactly what the other is saying?'

'Yes. So will you? Please?'

'When?'

'Now? It won't take very long—half an hour or so.'

And if she refused? It would look petty, wouldn't it? And, not wanting him to query any denial she might make, because he *would* query it, and any excuse would sound like just that, an excuse, she gave a reluctant nod. She could be entirely businesslike about this, couldn't she? It was, after all, *business*. 'All right.'

'Thank you. And knowing from past experience that end-of-filming parties tend to go on longer than is wise, I thought it best to see him now, instead of in the morning.' He smiled again, inviting her to share his joke.

She didn't want to share jokes, so she gave what she hoped was a cool smile. 'Because everyone will be hung over? You make it sound like an orgy.'

'No, just people telling each other how great they were, how good the film is going to be, drinking too much.'

'Now who's sounding cynical?'

He gave a comical little shrug. 'It's a cynical business.' His head on one side, he asked softly, 'Still feeling used?'

'No,' she denied stiffly.

'Good. I'll pay—for the interpreting,' he added quickly, an irrepressible laugh escaping him.

Opening her mouth to tell him that he didn't need to, feeling a fool, wishing she knew how to cope with him, she closed it again as she remembered the state of her finances, remembered she was being businesslike, and he laughed. 'That's it, Paris, never give anything for nothing.'

'Is that your philosophy?'

'Sure.'

She didn't somehow think it was, any more than it was usually her own, but needs must when the Devil drives. And was *this* why he was being so nice to her? Because he needed a favour? Hating herself for being such a pessimist, she quickly finished her coffee. 'I'll go up and get my coat.'

'Good girl.' Standing, he returned his chair to its rightful place. 'I'll wait for you in the foyer.'

The meeting didn't take long, just a preliminary discussion, and then an agreement to meet in London at the beginning of December. They all smiled, shook hands, and walked out into the cold, starry night.

'Want to walk for a bit? Look in the shops?'

'Oh, no, I don't think so,' she said hurriedly. 'I'll go on back, I think.'

He caught her hand, turned her to face him. 'Don't be a spoil-sport. I want you to help me choose something.'

'Why?' she asked bluntly.

He grinned. 'Because you have such excellent taste.' Without giving her another chance to refuse, he tucked their linked hands into his pocket. 'Shops are still open, aren't they?'

'Yes, they usually close about eight.' Not sure how to extricate herself without looking a fool, she allowed herself to be led towards the railway crossing. Was this another little game? She couldn't think of any other reason why he might want her company, and the feel of his warm fingers on hers was bittersweet. Nice, comforting, she admitted, and she tried very hard to be amused, philosophical, and couldn't. She was horrified to discover that, even knowing that it meant nothing to him, she didn't want this little interlude to end. Wanted to curl her fingers with his, not leave them lying lax. And he would feel the tension in her, wouldn't he? And then he would wonder. Trying to rationalise it to herself, for her own peace of mind, she wondered if it was simply caused by confusion. For two weeks they'd been sniping at each other, and now, suddenly, he was being nice. A different Oliver. Someone boyish and charming...

When he nudged her to capture her wandering attention, she gave a little start, stared round her in surprise, almost as though unsure where on earth she was, what she was doing.

'What do you think?' he asked.

'Mmm?' Forcing herself to concentrate, she stared into the window in front of them and the bright array of scarves displayed. Expensive scarves, she registered. Pure silk.

'Think my mum would like one?'

'Mum?' she echoed stupidly.

He turned his head, gave her an underbrowed glance. 'You said that as though you didn't think I could possibly have a mother.'

'Did I? Sorry.' With a faint smile, she turned to stare back into the window. 'It's just that it sounded so—ordinary. Oliver Darke with a mum.'

'I *am* ordinary.'

'Nonsense. What's she like? Dark? Fair?'

'Fair—to greying,' he grinned.

'That one.' She pointed. 'Pink.'

'Oh.' He sounded disappointed. 'Not that bright greeny thing?'

'No. Don't you like pink?'

'No.'

Diverted from her silent brooding, she asked curiously, 'Why?'

'Too bland.'

'That's no answer. What's she like? Elegant? Dumpy? What?'

'Dumpy?' he exclaimed. 'Good God, no!' Pursing his lips, he stared thoughtfully at nothing. 'Elegant,' he finally pronounced.

Like her son. 'And does she wear bright colours?'

He looked confused, then shook his head. 'She wears black—sometimes. Grey...'

'Then definitely the pink. Believe me,' she insisted. 'That particular shade of green is very difficult to wear. And it's not entirely pink,' she encouraged, 'it has shadings of grey.'

'But I don't *like* pink.'

With an unwilling laugh, and feeling helplessly exasperated, she tried to tug him inside. '*You* won't have to wear it.'

Halting her, holding her back, he peered down into her face. 'Did my kissing you upset you so very much? Is that's what's wrong?'

'Nothing's wrong!' she exclaimed quickly. 'And of course it didn't upset me. It was just a kiss, for goodness' sake! I have been kissed before, you know!' But not like that. Never like that.

'Yes, I imagine you have,' he agreed quietly.

Fool, Paris, fool! Pull yourself together. You *can't* be affected by him, you don't *like* actors, remember? It was utterly absurd, this awareness, and just because he was being nice to her... With an abrupt little movement, she led the way into the shop, leaving him no choice but to follow.

He bought the pink scarf for his mother, and, not entirely to be thwarted in his choice, bought the bright green one for his sister. 'She's dark,' he explained, as though that were answer enough.

Making a supreme effort, she asked brightly, 'You only have the one sister?'

'Yes, and two delightful nephews. And a brother-in-law, of course, and a dad, who, like you, is *entirely* unimpressed by my lofty status.'

She smiled, because that was what he expected, tried not to be delighted by this brief glimpse of the man behind the mask. She would treat him as a *friend*, she decided as they began to walk back to the hotel, putting nonsensical thoughts out of her head. A laudable intention that he immediately thwarted.

In a patch of shadow, he gently halted her and stared down into her face. 'You don't need to get any shopping?'

Wary again, worried, she shook her head. 'No, I bought some things for my friends the other day.'

'And do you always question things, Paris?' he asked, his voice still incredibly gentle. 'Doesn't spontaneity ever feature in your life?'

'Yes, of course it does.' He wasn't touching her, preventing her from moving, but the will-power needed to walk seemed to have gone, and that same sliding, blurring sensation was affecting her again, making her heart race, her throat dry.

'But not with me? Because I'm an actor, is that it? And little Paris Colby doesn't like actors? Or is it,' he continued softly, 'that you know as well as I that all our arguments, our inability to keep a civil tongue in our heads, is another name for awareness? Chemistry?'

'No. I mean, it isn't...' Her voice barely audible, she continued to stare up at him, noted the way the distant street-lamp haloed his hair, deepened the planes and angles of his face.

'Isn't it? Not an unwillingness to admit it? Recognise it for what it is?'

'Oliver...'

'Shh.' Putting his finger across her mouth, a finger that was gentle, yet seemed to burn, he continued, 'You, because of my profession, and me, because I'm always reluctant to say something that might be misconstrued, or later need to be retracted?'

'Then why are you...?'

'Saying it now? Because I think I was wrong about you; because I like you, admire you. And because...'

'You're afraid to trust people? Because of who you are?'

'Not afraid,' he denied. 'Reluctant, and if I've been less than generous, I'm sorry.' He smiled, removed his finger, and briefly replaced it with his mouth. 'Come on, you're shivering.'

Yes, but not from cold.

'I've become too cynical, too suspicious,' he murmured as he wrapped a casual arm round her shoulders, urged her into motion. 'Forgotten how to relax.' With an odd sigh, he hugged her briefly to his side.

And she was the one who'd been chosen to remind him? Was she supposed to be *honoured*? There was a light on in one of the trailers, she saw—probably the technicians holding a card school. Desperate for anything to distract her mind, because she didn't really know what he meant, what he was saying, she stared frantically at all that they passed. Noticed what cars were in the car park, saw that the glass doors into the foyer needed cleaning, and if he was saying what he seemed to be saying, then what? She didn't *want* to get involved with another actor.

Obediently climbing the stairs at his urging, she registered the individual voices sounding from the bar, smiled absently at the raucous laughter.

'Ready for the fray?' Oliver asked. 'You *are* coming, you know.'

'Am I?' Staring up at him, searching his face, such an impossibly handsome face that made anything she might think, feel, seem impossible, yet needing to clarify something, anything, she opened her mouth and closed it helplessly when he smiled, shook his head.

'Not now. And don't look so *worried*,' he reproved humorously. 'We'll talk later. Party first, because it's traditional! And you must never go to a party with a feeling of reluctance.'

'Mustn't I?'

'No. Anticipation, as in all things, my dear Paris, is the key to enjoyment.'

'Is it?'

'Yes. And I haven't spent the last half-hour or so dragging you round the shops to no point!' Ignoring her puzzled look, he tugged her towards the doorway.

Giving in to the inevitable, she allowed herself to be ushered inside. Henry was holding forth, laughingly telling everyone of their adventures.

'...and she may look like a stick insect, but believe me, that is one bossy, determined lady!'

There was the sound of laughter, and she glanced at Oliver, gave him a wry smile. It hadn't been said maliciously, only in fun, but being compared to a stick insect... 'At the agency where I work,' she said softly, 'I'm affectionately known as Hattie, as in hat rack—at least, I hope it's affectionately.'

'I'd bet on it,' he returned just as softly. Capturing her hand, he squeezed it and then led her forward.

A genuinely kind gesture, she wondered, or a last bit of insurance that she would remain a fan for life? That she would always, ever after, say he was a kind man? Don't be cynical, Paris. No. But he *was* an actor. And actors—acted.

He released her hand, pushed her forward, and the noise and laughter suddenly stopped, cut off in mid-flow. Astonished, she stared at the group, and the group stared back. Hovering in acute embarrassment, not knowing what on *earth* was going on, she stared at them all in turn, and then George stepped forward, grasped her hand and pulled her into the centre of the now-silent crew. He picked up a gaily wrapped package from the bar, and solemnly handed it to her.

'To say thank you,' he explained. 'It's from all of us, for your help, your kindness...'

Bewildered, feeling awkward and unsure, she stared round her at the expectant, smiling faces. 'But I didn't *do* anything!'

There was a general laugh of disbelief.

'But I didn't!' she insisted.

'You came when you didn't want to—oh, yes, I know all about Japan. You soothed Melissa...'

Not daring to glance at Oliver, she hung her head, stared at the pink bow on the present.

'You kept all the locals happy...'

'No...'

'Yes. We had absolutely no trouble with anyone—spectators, officials...'

'But that wasn't because of me,' she protested.

'Yes it was! Despite the weather, my bad temper, Melissa's awkwardness...'

'Oliver's bloodymindedness,' Oliver put in with a grin.

'...for the first time that I can remember,' George continued determinedly, 'we had an interpreter who soothed, gentled, didn't put the locals' backs up by being patronising, officious, charmed the mayor, the local police-force, owners of fields which turned into a quagmire...'

'Oh, stop,' she pleaded, her cheeks hot. 'I only did what you paid me to do.'

'Yes?' he queried, one eyebrow cocked. 'Did we pay you to hump props? Untangle cables? Act as unofficial seamstress when Melissa complained that her dress didn't fit? Washer-upper...'

'But only because I wasn't doing anything else at the time!'

There was a roar of laughter that she didn't in the least understand, and she looked helplessly into the sea of faces that surrounded her.

'The last interpreter I worked with,' George explained, 'didn't have much to do on occasion either, but no way would she dirty her hands with the washing-up!'

'You don't dirty hands with washing-up!' someone retorted humorously. 'You get them clean!'

More laughter.

'She had her job description, and, by God, was she sticking to it!' George insisted. 'She put up the backs of everyone! We had spectators wandering all over the set— which it wasn't her job to clear! It was a nightmare! If we'd had her,' he continued more softly, 'I doubt this film would ever have been finished. And I suspect you know how important it was to me, don't you?'

'Yes, but...'

'So, we'd like you to accept this little gift by way of thanks.'

Choked, her eyes prickling, and not knowing what on earth to say, she gave a tremulous smile and began to unwrap the little parcel. It was perfume. Expensive perfume, in the most gorgeous crystal bottle. 'Oh,' she exclaimed. Glancing up, her blue eyes misty, she gave another wobbly smile. 'Thank you. It's lovely.'

'We didn't know what to get, and we were a bit limited because we had to find a shop where the assistant spoke English,' George grinned. 'A shop very quickly,' he added, 'while Oliver kept you out of the way. Which meant either the *perfumaria* or the camping shop, and we didn't think you'd want a tent!'

'No,' she denied helplessly. So that was why he'd dragged her round the town, as he put it. Not for her company. But then why had he said all those other things? Realising that they were still all waiting, she managed a smile. 'Thank you. Thank you all. Very much.'

'Right, what's everyone drinking?'

Perched on a high stool at the bar, nursing her glass of white wine, her eyes on the bottle of perfume, only vaguely aware of the noise and laughter around her, she felt a fraud. She hadn't done anything special, in fact most of the time she'd been as irritable as everyone else.

'Don't look so worried,' Oliver reproved from beside her.

Glancing up, she gave a faint smile, sadder than it need have been. 'I didn't really deserve a present.'

'Of course you did.'

'I wasn't very nice to you.'

'My back's broad,' he grinned.

'Yes.' And it had been kind of him to keep her occupied... But why was he being so nice to her *now*? Because he was nice to everyone? Although, he hadn't been especially nice a few days ago. Because he was working, and now he wasn't? And why on earth couldn't she just accept it in the spirit it was no doubt meant? Because she was used to the acting profession being light-hearted and shallow? Yet that couldn't be true of all of them, any more than it was true that all models were brainless bimbos or accountants wore glasses. And did it even matter if he was being shallow? But he had said that they would talk... Desperately pushing it from her mind, she stared round her. 'What happened to Henry?' she asked in surprise.

'Gone to bed with a hot toddy. He doesn't like parties. Got lots of exciting work lined up when you get back?'

'Not to my knowledge; no doubt William will inform me differently,' she smiled. Hoped William would inform her differently; with all these debts to pay off, she needed as much work as she could get. And if Athena, as she suspected, came out with yet more troubles for her to solve... Her unconscious sigh sounded almost despairing.

'Problems?' he asked softly as he leaned on the bar beside her.

His dark brown eyes were kind, interested. Or was it an expression he used in his profession? Able to turn it off and on... Oh, stop it, Paris!

'No,' she denied, 'I expect I'm just tired, and a little overwhelmed by everyone's kindness.' Especially yours. And a little apprehensive about the reason for my sister's visit.

'That makes it sound as though you aren't used to people being kind.'

'No, yes, oh, I don't know.' She smiled, more naturally this time. 'And you? Back to your filming?'

''Fraid so.'

'Don't you enjoy it?'

'Enjoy it?' he queried thoughtfully. 'Yes, I suppose I do—the working part, anyway. I don't entirely enjoy the—trappings,' he added with a rather cynical twist to his mouth.

Didn't he? Entirely the opposite view of her brother-in-law and his entourage. They seemed to enjoy the trappings more than the work! 'And where is the lovely Melissa?' she asked before she could stop herself. 'Doesn't she attend these bashes?'

'Afraid I might kiss her again?' he teased, and then laughed. 'The lovely Melissa,' he explained drily, 'has already gone. Whisked away the moment she got back to the hotel.'

'Not quite the mom——'

'Paris,' he warned softly. 'I shall begin to think you *are* jealous.'

'Hmph.' He was probably intending to see her back in England. He probably... 'What happens if George needs to do some more takes?' she asked determinedly.

He gave her a sly grin. 'How's your acting?'

Startled into a little grunt of laughter, she shook her head.

'No? Not even a love-scene?' Raising and lowering his eyebrows in comical suggestion, totally unaware of the little seed of yearning he unleashed, he reluctantly, or apparently reluctantly, moved aside to make room for one of the cameramen who wanted to chat with her about Spain, where he would be going next, and so it went on, and her intention of only having one drink was forgotten. Time was marching on, wasn't it? Time for her to meet someone, fall in love, marry and have children... Don't be so maudlin! Defiantly determined to enjoy herself, drinking all that she was given without a thought for any possible hangover, several hours later she was rather hazily astonished at how much she was succeeding. It was rather nice to be the centre of attention for a change, even if they were members of the dreaded profession. She might also have been very surprised to learn that it wasn't because she was the only female present that everyone made a fuss of her, but because she was genuinely liked, was excellent company, that she had a fund of hilarious anecdotes about her work as a translator and was a very good raconteur. She was also an excellent mimic, and rather naughtily gave impressions, not only of George's brother, which had the tubby director in stitches, but of Melissa, whom she had off to a 'T'. She glanced rather slyly at Oliver to see how he was taking it, and found that he was laughing as much as everyone else. But looking at him had been a mistake, because it reminded her of her of what he had said, of her own amorous yearnings, and she suddenly found that she wanted to slide her arms round that strong neck, fit her body against his, feel his warmth, his... With a little shudder she finished her drink too quickly, felt momentarily ill, and within seconds Oliver was by her side.

'Time to go,' he said softly.

'I'm all right...'

'No, you aren't,' he said gently. 'Come on.'

'You aren't responsible...' she began, hazily registered his determination, and squinted down at her watch. 'It's gone two!' she exclaimed in surprise.

'Yes.'

With a rather bewildered air she glanced round, saw that only the stalwarts were left. George, Oliver, a couple of the lighting experts, and herself. She had no memory of the others leaving, and that was a bit worrying.

When Oliver gently grasped her arm to help her down, she thought about shaking him off, glanced at him, and gave in. Her earlier euphoria had definitely changed to a vague feeling of distress. The room also seemed to have taken on a slight list.

Actually remembering to pick up her bag and the precious bottle of perfume, and, with Oliver helping her, she began the slow walk to the exit.

'I *can* manage, you know,' she said with marvellous dignity.

'Mmm,' he agreed with some amusement as he scooped up their coats and his own parcels from the chair by the door.

'There's really no need for you to accompany me.'

He quirked an eyebrow at her.

'Anyone would think I was drunk.'

'Anyone would be right,' he murmured. 'Come on, funny lady; independence is all very well, but I'd *hate* to be responsible for you falling down the stairwell!'

'I've never fallen down a stairwell in my life!'

He laughed.

Strangely, the corridor to her room seemed to have lengthened, taken on distorted proportions, and when her key transformed itself into an unwieldy object that wouldn't fit the keyhole she was rather glad of his assistance. And all would have been well if Oliver hadn't needed to come in to leave her coat, if she hadn't forgotten to unplug her hairdryer, the flex of which still trailed across the carpet, because then she wouldn't have caught her foot in it. Oliver wouldn't have needed to try and save her, and they wouldn't both have sprawled on to the wide, soft, very, very welcome bed.

Her nose almost touching his, her eyes definitely unfocused at such close quarters, she stared at his lashes. They looked very long, and thick. 'Thank you,' she said solemnly.

'You're welcome. And now I must go.'

'Yes.'

He didn't move an inch. 'I will swing my feet to the floor, stand, make my way to my own room...' There was a little pause while he stared rather searchingly at her, and the alcoholic haze fled on silent wings. Excitement took its place.

He smiled, that delightful Oliver smile, and the most delicious pain slid down to her stomach.

'Did you have your teeth fixed?' she asked foolishly.

He blinked. 'Pardon?'

'Expensive dental work?'

'Dental work?'

'Mmm.'

He frowned. 'I don't think so.'

'Oh. Plastic surgery?'

With a funny little shake of his head, amusement lurking in his beautiful eyes, he denied, 'No. No, I definitely didn't have plastic surgery. I would have remembered.'

'Yes, something like that you would definitely have remembered.'

'Yes. So I couldn't have had it, could I?'

'No.'

They smiled at each other.

'I'm sorry I kissed you in the car,' he apologised solemnly.

'Are you?'

'Yes. I've been thinking about it all evening. Shouldn't have done it.'

'No.'

'Then.'

'Sorry?' she queried.

'Then,' he repeated. 'Should have done it later.'

'You did,' she pointed out dreamily. 'On the stairs. In the street.'

'So I did.'

'Why?'

'Why?' His eyes a great deal clearer than her own, a half-smile on his mouth, he said softly, 'Because I wanted to.'

'Did you?'

'Yes. The way I do right now.' Rolling forward a fraction, he touched his mouth to hers. Just touched, soft as a butterfly wing, and heat spiralled through her, a sliding, spreading feeling of—desire.

His tongue touched fleetingly against her lower lip, and she groaned, moved one arm across him, touched his strong back, wanted to immerse herself in the scent of him, the texture, touch that soft skin, inhale the fresh smell of his hair. Forever.

One strong hand reached for her hip, urged it closer, halted, and he drew back to stare down to see what was digging into his stomach. Removing her bag, and the perfume that she still held clutched to her chest, he reached behind him to put them on the floor, smiled, drew her more firmly into his embrace, and the kiss deepened, became magical, and as his thighs touched hers, her throat dried, and a tremor of excitement, need, shook her. A small part of her—the sober, sensible part of her—said, No, don't be a fool, but the rest of her, the soft, compliant, needful part of her, said, Yes, yes, yes. Please.

Moving her hand up to his nape, a movement that was dreamlike, special, she trailed her fingers through hair that felt like silk, and as he continued to kiss her, softly, almost experimentally, learning her secrets, her thoughts, a tiny part of her mind asked, Is this a role he's playing? A part he's played before? And if she said 'cut' would he stop, blink, roll away? But she wasn't really listening to her mind, and she didn't want to say 'cut'. Tomorrow there would be regret, possibly shame, embarrassment, but not now. Now she wanted it all. As, it appeared, did he. Because he'd had too much to drink and had forgotten who she was?

'Paris?' he whispered against her mouth, a tiny breath of sound, audible only to her. A whisper laced with laughter.

'Yes?'

'I'm not entirely sober.'

'No.'

'And, stupid as it might sound, I feel extraordinarily aroused, and I want to make love to you.'

'Yes. Why might it sound stupid?'

'Because you don't like me.'

Oh, Oliver, I do, I do, I do.

Moving her fingers to his face, she traced his eyebrows, his classical nose, the side of his mouth where it still rested against hers. 'I changed my mind,' she murmured. 'I like you fine.'

She felt him smile and touched one foot to his calf, began to rub it up and down. 'But I'm only little Paris Colby, and tomorrow you will be sorry.'

'Never. I like little Paris Colby. She has a sexy mouth.'

Did she? That was nice. She didn't know how her dress had become rucked up above her thighs, only knew that it was, knew that one warm palm rested there, and, fair being fair, she undid the buttons on his shirt, slid her own hand inside to his warm back. He shivered.

'Your hand's cold.'

'Sorry,' she apologised huskily. 'Want me to move it?'

'Yes,' he agreed thickly, 'but it might be wiser to leave it where it is.' Gathering her closer, he began to kiss her again, not gently now, not softly, but with warmth and passion and need, and, as he kissed her, he moved her over on to her back, tangled his fingers in her hair, rested his body against hers, stared down into her blue eyes and, as if he only then fully realised what he was doing, he paused, sighed, allowed his body to slump, yet one hand still remained clenched rather tightly in her hair.

Quivering, still keyed up, she stared worriedly into his eyes. 'What?' she whispered huskily.

'Nothing,' he denied.

'Oliver!' she protested.

Sounding almost regretful, he repeated softly, 'Nothing.'

'It must be something...'

'No. I told you. Just leave it, Paris, there's a good girl.'

'But you can't just turn it off and on like a tap...' she began confusedly, and then remembered that he could. That was exactly what he could do. 'You forgot who I was, didn't you?' she asked quietly.

'What?' Giving her a puzzled frown, he shook his head. 'No, I forgot who I was. And I sometimes yearn...' He began to move, and she held him still. Didn't *want* his warmth removed from her just yet. She knew she was being stupid, but alcohol had clouded her reason. Dulled sense, enhanced sensation.

One hand still crumpling his sleeve, the other at his back, she whispered, 'What do you yearn?' His breathing was still slightly laboured, his muscles tensed, as though he held himself on a tight rein—and the still swollen warmth against her groin was impossible to ignore. 'Is it Melissa?'

'Melissa?'

'Yes. Is it because she went back?' Edging the material of his shirt higher, she flattened her hand against his warm back, slid it round to rub his nipple with unconscious provocation, until he groaned, grasped her fingers, stilled the movement.

'Dear God, Paris...'

'*Is* it Melissa? Because you're involved with her?'

'No, I told you.'

'I want you,' she whispered, her eyes wide with unconscious entreaty, and didn't care that she was being blatant. Her body was so warm, needing, his thighs were hard, his body arousing... And he must want her, too, his body said so. 'You'll be leaving tomorrow,' she murmured sadly. 'I won't see you any more.'

'Do you want to?'

'Yes.' Her breathing accelerated, her heart a triple hammer that echoed in her ears, her temples; she moved her hips a fraction, deliberately enticed, and his eyes were darker, his body warmer, his mouth more... With a groan, she arched her neck, closed her eyes.

CHAPTER FIVE

'PARIS...' His voice was thicker, and his breathing wasn't any too steady either, and then his mouth was against hers, his hand a brand that burnt into her thigh, and he was...and then he...and she began melting, from the inside. Strength left her knees, her arms, her eyelids, and she felt boneless, ensorcelled, as his mouth and then his hands made music not heard this side of heaven. His body was a warm, heavy weight, not hurting, not uncomfortable, and when he moved his hands, allowed his palms to gently frame her jaw, fingers touching behind her ears, she freed his shirt entirely, touched her hands to his warm, naked back, revelled in the feel of smooth flesh, revelled in sensations too exquisite to define. Practised, her mind tried to whisper, and if kissing her made her feel mindless, just his mouth touching hers made her thoughts spiral out of control, then his hard frame against hers was something else again. She felt drugged.

She protested when he moved, but not when he stripped her of her dress; she helped him when he unclipped her bra, groaned in pleasure when he gently, seductively, pleasurably, removed her hold-up stockings. Not a word was exchanged as he slid his mouth from her ankle to her knee, to her groin, slipped his thumb between the lace of her panties, and then slowly returned his mouth to hers, teased her willing lips apart, touched his tongue to parted teeth—and surrender was as inevitable as it was desired. He was gentle, exciting, sure. No messy fumblings, no awkwardness, and, when he had loved her to the mindless exclusion of all else, he curved her warmly against his side, pulled the cover over them, and urged softly, 'Go to sleep.'

'I don't want to,' she mumbled. Pleasurably languorous, she wanted to talk, whisper things to him, explain how she felt, touch him, arouse him again... I have Oliver Darke in my bed, she told herself as she sensuously smoothed her hand across his ribcage; I have just experienced the most beautiful, most fulfilling, exciting moment of my life, and he wants me to go to sleep. Her lids impossibly weighted, her breathing slowing, drifting on a tide of sensation, a soft smile on her face, denial forgotten, she did as she was told.

Noise woke her, a discordant rattle, whether outside the hotel or in she didn't know, only that light was hurting her eyes. Squinting, she registered sunlight through undrawn curtains. Sunlight? And then she registered the warmth of another body, an arm that was a heavy weight across her waist, and sleep fled as quickly as it had engulfed her. Moving only her eyes, she stared in horror at tousled blond hair, a stubbled jaw... And to her utter dismay, she had utter, total recall. She'd *seduced* him! He hadn't been *unwilling* exactly, and he wasn't the sort of man to be coerced, but... Oh, Paris, what have you done? And what in God's name did she say when he woke up? 'Hello, dear, have a good sleep?' She could feel a little bubble of hysteria at the back of her throat, feel the desire to laugh and keep on laughing; she briefly considered fleeing, but where to? This was *her* room, and maybe she made some small sound, alerted him, because one brown eye suddenly opened.

He stared at her, blinked, and then he smiled. 'Oh, dear.'

'Yes,' she whispered stupidly.

'Good?' Taking in her worried face, he queried comically, 'Not so good?'

'Oh, Oliver. I was drunk!'

His smile widened. 'I wasn't,' he said softly.

'I *know*.' Was he regretting it? she asked herself feverishly. Remembering all those other women? Women who used him... 'I'm sorry,' she blurted. Her face flaming, she jerked her head away. She felt so *stupid*. Wished she could get up, run away, hide. She'd practically *begged* him! And his naked thigh was pressing against her own, and there was a funny little flutter in her stomach. Nerves? Or desire? His thigh shifted, and she drew in a snatched breath, swallowed hard, tried to ease free.

'Cramp,' he murmured teasingly.

'Oh.'

'Headache?'

She gave a jerky nod, then winced. 'And I'm not *ever* going to drink again.'

'Didn't affect your performance any...'

'Oliver!' she protested.

He laughed, reached out, pulled her back against him, nuzzled the warmth of her neck. 'Paris, Paris,' he began soothingly.

'Oh, don't,' she begged, her voice muffled by his shoulder, and so very aware of their nakedness, of his warm thigh against her own, his arm across her waist, she struggled to find words to make it right. 'Please don't say anything else,' she begged. 'I feel mortified enough as it is.'

'Mortified?'

Hearing a different note in his voice, she raised her head to look at him, then wished she hadn't. His eyes

still warm from sleep, his face so—rakishly attractive,
she swallowed, nodded.

'You regret it? Is that what you're saying?' he asked
gently.

'Well, of course I regret it! Don't you?'

He shook his head.

'You don't?' she asked worriedly.

'No. You think I took advantage of you, is that it?'

'No! Of course I don't think that!' she denied fret-
fully. 'And that wasn't very gallant.'

'No. Nor is your...'

'My what?' she demanded.

He shook his head, refused to explain. Because it
wasn't worth even discussing? Because it hadn't been
the most exciting moment in his life? Well, of course it
hadn't, she told herself impatiently as she continued to
stare at him, into brown eyes that held an expression she
couldn't quite identify; he probably did it all the
time...and she wanted to cry, because she felt so foolish.
Wanted to be held, reassured, wanted to shove him off
and on to the floor. Didn't know why she didn't. Pride?
A pretence that she didn't care? But she did. So very
much. She'd never gone in for casual sex, never leapt in
and out of bed as the mood took her. Never slept with
someone on such short acquaintance. She'd had two
lovers in her twenty-nine years, and both times she had
thought herself in love. But they hadn't felt like this.
She hadn't felt anxious, frightened—so very aching. So
very—stupid. And now he would think...probably *did*
think, and she had no idea what to say, how to make it
right, and when he reached out, touched his fingers to
her face, she flinched, turned her face away, didn't see
his speculative look as he allowed his hand to drop.

Staring down at the well-muscled forearm that lay across the covers, she moved her eyes to his hand. A beautiful hand, strong, tender... With a small, twisted smile she closed her eyes, hiding the embarrassment that lingered there. So what happened now?

She had wanted him to love her, give in to the emotions that had buffeted her; she had let him love her as she had probably wanted him to love her from the moment he had stepped down from his private plane. Loved him back with all the passion she was capable of—because drink had clouded her reason, but not her desire. And, to him, it probably meant less than nothing. No, not less than *nothing* perhaps, but nothing out of the ordinary. And would this one experience have to last her the rest of her life? A beautiful memory of how it could be? And, when they met later, would he just say, 'Hi'? Smile, go on his merry way? Hi, she thought she could cope with, but if he tried to make her feel cheap...

It's just chemistry, she tried to tell herself, strong attraction, a desire to have something special. On her part, anyway. And it had been something special. Nothing would probably ever be as special again... Oh, will you shut up, Paris! He made love to you, you made love to him. It happened all the time, all over the world—she just wished that reducing it to its lowest common denominator actually worked! Wished that Oliver could feel as she did. Only he didn't, did he? Couldn't possibly... *Probably* did not feel as she did... Possibly, he...

Agitated, not even really knowing what she was doing, but remembering so *vividly* what he had said about other women, about how they... she thrust the covers aside, started to swing her legs free, and he grasped her arm, stayed her.

'Running away?' he asked softly. 'That won't solve anything.'

'I'm not running away,' she denied with shaken dignity, 'and there is nothing to solve. I just want to get up, forget it...'

'*Forget* it? You only wanted me because you were *drunk*? Is that what you're saying?'

Shocked, she twisted to face him. 'No! Of course that isn't what I'm saying!'

'Then what are you saying? Thanks, but now that I'm sober, no thanks?'

'No! Stop twisting things!' Needing to put space between them, she lunged for her robe that was lying on the dressing-table stool. Shrugging into it, feeling marginally more in control now that she was covered, she took a small breath and bravely tried again. 'I was only saying... Well, that you wouldn't have made love to me if I hadn't *forced* you.'

'Wouldn't I?'

Uncertain, she turned to stare at him doubtfully. Perhaps, after all...

'Why *did* you want to make love to me, Paris?'

'Why?' she echoed.

'Yes, why? Because I'm famous?'

'Famous? Don't be absurd. And I already told you after we—in the—I already told you I wasn't like that!'

'So you did.'

'Don't you believe me?' she asked unhappily.

Without immediately answering, he hauled himself up in the bed, leaned against the headboard, and, with his eyes on her face, almost as though he were trying to see a truth there, he asked, 'Then why the regret? It was a nice interlude, a——'

'I don't *believe* you!' she exclaimed tearfully. 'How can you even *ask* me that? I suppose next you'll want to know if I was bloody satisfied?'

'Were you?' he asked softly.

'Yes!'

'I'm very glad to hear it.'

'Stop it!' she cried. 'Stop it! Why are you *being* like this?'

'Because I'm beginning to wonder if I haven't been used,' he said quietly.

'Used? Oh, Oliver, no!' Reaching out, hesitantly touching him, she exclaimed even more worriedly, 'I was, am, *embarrassed*! I don't, I mean . . .'

'You don't normally leap in and out of bed as the fancy takes you?' he asked more gently.

'Yes. I mean, no.' With a helpless sigh, she just stared at him, and when he gave her a gentle smile, she smiled shyly back. 'I'm sorry.'

'So you should be.'

Feeling awkward and unsure of herself, she looked down, fiddled with the belt of her robe. We made love, she told herself, and she *still* didn't quite believe it. That she could have so far forgotten herself. And it had been so *perfect*! And now she was behaving like a frightened virgin, not like herself at all. She should have been blasé, pretended, and then maybe she could have carried it off—as she would have carried it off if it hadn't *mattered*. But if it hadn't mattered, she wouldn't have had him in her bed in the first place. With a sigh, she peeped at him, blushed faintly when he gave her a look that was—well, sexually blatant, caught sight of the clock and blurted stupidly, 'It's gone eight.'

'Has it?' he asked drily. 'And Paris Colby won't allow intimate discussions after eight o'clock in the morning? Some sort of watershed, is it?'

'No,' she mumbled, 'don't be silly. I just meant, if we wanted breakfast... And don't look at me like that! I only meant...you know I didn't mean—that!'

He chuckled, flung off the covers and, standing unashamedly naked, he stretched, yawned, and bent to pull on his trousers. 'Better?' he taunted softly, and she nodded, gave a shamefaced grin.

'I'm not used to...'

'I know,' he agreed gently. 'That's why I've forgiven you.'

'*Forgiven* me?'

'Mmm.'

'For what?' she asked, beginning to be justifiably incensed by his casual tone.

'Your—mortification, of course.' Scooping up his clothes, he made for the door, hesitated, came back and dropped a kiss on her surprised mouth. 'Don't be late for breakfast.'

Picking up her hairbrush, she threw it half-heartedly after him, and then just sat there with a silly smile on her face. Smoothing out the belt of her robe, amused warmth in her eyes, her smile even more foolish, she decided that maybe it was all right. Maybe. Her headache forgotten, she got up, wandered into the bathroom, caught sight of herself in the long mirror, and stuck out her tongue. So? she defiantly asked her reflection. We only made love. *Only*? That had never been *only*! And his behaviour implied that it would happen—again. That... Don't think ahead, Paris, she warned herself. Don't *anticipate*! No, but it was very hard not to. Still staring at herself, she tilted her head to one side. An ordinary face, a face smeared with last night's make-up, she noted ruefully, and eyes that looked—smug. You're a very silly girl, Paris Colby. Yes. And found she didn't in the least care.

You don't love him, she told herself, knowing she needed the warning, at least *trying* to be sensible. How could you? You don't even *know* him. Like him, yes, was delighted by him, and, remembering their love-making, she felt warmth flood through her. But if she hadn't had too much to drink, would he...? Shut up, Paris! Reaching for her toothbrush, she forced her mind into other channels. Like the knowledge that in a few hours Athena would be here.

By nine-thirty she was showered and changed—and was *still* having to force the silly smile off her face! But the memories of his lovemaking, his warmth, his teasing, gave her a warm glow inside, a feeling of—anticipation, and hoping, praying that nothing of this showed on her face, she walked with every appearance of composure down to the dining-room.

Aware of the buzz of conversation from inside the restaurant, wondering if she was first, or whether Oliver had beaten her to it, she took a deep breath, straightened her shoulders, and stepped inside. No Oliver, but Athena had already arrived—and was doing what she did best.

Unobserved for the moment, she tried to be objective as she watched her pretty sister hold court. A word here, a smile there, as she so easily, happily ensnared the film crew, the waiters who hovered, awaiting recognition. Even Henry looked adoring, and an absurd little dart of jealousy pierced her, only to be as hastily dismissed. They were alike—well, in so far as they had the same colouring, the same blue eyes—but everything about

Athena was brighter, better, more rounded. Her hair was curlier, her eyes bluer, her figure more shapely. Paris always felt like the copy that nature hadn't got quite right—but not today, and, determinedly forcing the black demon back where he belonged, knowing she was being stupid because, in reality, she was really rather proud of her sister's beauty, her popularity, she walked to meet her sister.

'Paris!' she exclaimed. Carelessly dismissing her court, arms theatrically wide, she hugged Paris as though she hadn't seen her for months.

Dismissing the possibly unworthy thought that such exuberance was for the crew's benefit, Paris returned the hug.

'Darling!' Athena purred extravagantly, 'I've been waiting for *hours*!'

'Don't exaggerate,' Paris smiled, 'if you'd been here hours you'd have been up banging on my door.' And wouldn't that have been a shock for everyone concerned?

'Don't be so practical,' she pouted, but there was a very odd glitter in her eyes that Paris definitely found worrying. 'And if you'd told me there were so many delicious men here——' she exaggerated, loud enough for everyone to hear '—I'd have been here days ago!'

'I know,' Paris grinned. 'That's why I didn't tell you.' Staring at her sister, trying to *concentrate*, not keep glancing at the doorway like an expectant child, she wondered again at the rather febrile gaiety that clung to Athena. Almost an air of anticipation. Automatically returning the smiles of the film crew, acknowledging their greetings, thanks, goodbyes, she steered her sister towards an empty table. 'Have you eaten?'

'Of course,' she murmured with an arch look, 'George invited me to sit with him. But I'll have another coffee with you, if you like.'

'Thank you,' Paris said drily. Ordering coffee and rolls from the smiling waiter, very well aware that *something* was troubling her pretty sister, Paris put her elbows on the table, rested her chin in her palms, and teased softly, 'So, to what *do* I owe the pleasure?'

'A stop-over! I told you, well, I told whoever answered the phone to me to tell you.'

'Stop-over to where?'

'The States, of course! And then I arrived just as everyone was leaving!'

'Mmm. What's wrong?' Paris asked quietly.

'Wrong?' she exclaimed with every appearance of astonishment. 'What should be wrong?'

'I don't know, but something is, almost as if you were waiting for something to happen.'

'Don't be silly. And *I'm* the one with the imagination, remember?' With a bright smile at the waiter as he carefully poured her coffee, she waited until he'd gone before resuming, 'Don't you want to know about the States?'

'Yes, of course I do. Er, you haven't burnt the flat down or something?' she pleaded with humorous hope of denial. 'Wrecked the car?'

'Of course I haven't! Do be serious!'

Not entirely comforted, but knowing from past experience that it was waste of time trying to get Athena to tell you something if she didn't want to, she smiled encouragingly. 'OK, tell me about the States. Chris has found work?'

'You don't need to sound so hopeful,' Athena reproved, 'but yes, he has! Isn't it marvellous? Only in a soap; it won't make his name, of course, but quite lucrative. And don't pretend to be sorry to see me go, because we both know it won't be true!' she concluded with the teasing smile that seemed to captivate everyone she met.

'And you naturally didn't want to go without saying goodbye,' Paris murmured with her own brand of teasing.

'No. So here I am! And...'

'Yes, here you are.' Hating herself for being so suspicious, she added quietly, 'How?'

'How?'

'Yes, as in how did you afford the fare?'

'Paris! I thought you'd be pleased to see me!'

'I am.'

'And it might be ages before we meet again!'

'Yes.'

'You're always so practical!'

'Someone has to be,' she reproved gently.

'Why? It takes all the fun out of things!' With a rather sly smile, she added, 'Did you know that Rupert got married?'

'No, and you can take that look off your face; I am not brokenhearted, nor do I mind. I hope he will be very happy.'

A sulky look to her mouth, Athena complained, 'Don't you even want to know who it is?'

'Not particularly.'

'It could have been you,' she burst out, 'if you hadn't been so picky!'

'Picky not to want to be two-timed?' Paris asked gently.

'It didn't mean anything!'

'No, I know, but her father was a producer, and Rupert wanted to further his career. Is that who he married?'

'Yes. And you let her win!'

Reaching across the table, she touched her sister's hand. 'It wasn't a question of winning,' she pointed out gently. 'And if I'd really loved him... I wasn't that hurt, you know. Or at least——' she qualified '—I soon got over it, so I couldn't have been. And it wasn't really my scene. All that backbiting, jealousy, the petty squabbles. I'm not like you, Athena, I don't enjoy...'

'Tinsel town!' Athena scoffed.

'No. I like being independent, like to direct my own life, not be an extension of someone else's...' Ha, ha, ha, really directed it last night, didn't you? Glancing quickly down, not wanting Athena to see the smile in her eyes and wonder at it, as she would, she went on hastily, 'I don't want the things you want, enjoy the things you enjoy,' she resumed quietly. Gently touching her sister's hand, she asked softly, 'Are you happy, 'Thena?'

'Of course I'm happy! I know you don't like Chris...'

'I don't like what he's done to you,' she corrected.

'I know, I know,' Athena cut in impatiently. 'Made me hard, made me selfish! But he didn't! I was always that! Always knew what I wanted. You just wouldn't see it. Tried to make me like you...'

'No! That's not fair. I only tried to give you a set of values...'

'*Your* values. Not mine! I know you thought you had to be a mummy figure when Mum died, but...'

'Oh, Athena, I didn't, just tried to guide you, help...'

'Well, don't let's argue about it now,' she broke in impatiently, 'be glad for me, I'll be happy out there.

Lots of sunshine, house with a pool, parties... And don't pull faces! I couldn't bear your life, always working...'
Breaking off, she bit her lip, and, Athena being Athena, was immediately on the defensive. 'Anyway, it's your own fault! You shouldn't lend me money! I keep telling you!'

'I should leave you to roam the streets? Live in a cardboard box?'

With a little giggle, she summoned up a smile. 'I wouldn't, you know.'

'No,' Paris sighed. 'I do know. You'd inveigle some other poor idiot into giving you things. Born with too much charm, that's your trouble.'

'And you were born without enough. I do love you, Paris, it's just that...'

'I'm so practical.'

'Yes. Friends again?'

'Friends,' Paris agreed, as she always agreed, ever since they'd been children. It was wrong, of course, but so very hard to deny Athena what she wanted. Silly to feel responsible for her; she was all grown up now, able to direct her own life, but old habits died hard. 'You really do want to go to the States? I mean, if you didn't...'

'I do,' Athena said firmly. 'And,' she added, bright triumph in her face, 'I'm going to have a screen-test! *That's* what I came to tell you! I might be able to get a walk-on part in Chris's soap, and...'

'Screen test?' Paris echoed in dismay.

'Yes! So, not only a famous brother-in-law, but you might soon have a famous sister!'

'And it's really what you want?' she asked hollowly. Was that what she'd been discussing with George? Telling him, hoping for...

'Oh, Paris, don't look like that! I *want* it!'

Yes. Finding a smile, nodding, accepting it, and, in truth, rather relieved that all this would be taking place in America, she asked, 'How long can you stay?'

'Not long.' Glancing at her watch, she murmured, 'Half an hour or so. The hire-car's coming back for me at ten. I only popped in to see you, say hello really, tell you my news, and that I've left the flat all nice and tidy, and...'

'Hire-car?' Paris exclaimed in horror. 'Oh, Athena. How on earth did you afford a car *and* the fare? I didn't think you had any money.' If she'd lied to her, used Paris's savings when all the time she had money of her own...

Affecting deafness, Athena got to her feet, forcing Paris to do the same. 'I really have to g... *There* he is!' she exclaimed in satisfaction.

Bewildered, Paris turned to follow the direction of her glance, saw Oliver, began to smile, registered what Athena had said, and asked quietly, 'You know him?'

'Of course I know him.' Her sister forgotten, her smile wide, enchanting, she fluttered across the room like a pretty butterfly.

Staring after her, a little frown in her eyes, Paris tried to dismiss the thought that her sister's air of anticipation had been because of Oliver, and couldn't. Had she known he was here? How? Because George, or one of the crew had told her? Or had she known already, and *that* was why she'd come? Not to see her sister, but to see Oliver. Athena had never mentioned him—but that didn't mean she didn't know him... And Oliver was the highest star in the current firmament, and Athena only liked the best.

Hating herself for her suspicions, the twist of jealousy she felt, she stood like a fool, watched her sister smile seductively at him, and then frowned, because he didn't smile back. Men *always* smiled at Athena.

She couldn't hear what they said to each other, only knew they were saying something, and then Athena slid her hands up Oliver's chest, stood on tiptoe as if to press a kiss to his mouth, and Paris felt that awful sliding feeling in her stomach, that twist of pain. Oh, no. Please, no, I saw him first... Horrified at the way her thoughts were going, what she had almost said, as though he were a piece of property, she went to turn away, then saw him grasp Athena's wrists and forcibly remove her arms from his neck. Athena pouted, scathing, almost. Puzzled, and very well aware that they must know each other if they were *arguing*, she continued to watch them, and then he glanced at Paris, said something to her sister, and began striding across to where she stood.

'Good God, Paris, what did you *tell* her?'

'What?' she asked blankly.

'It was bad enough being *seen*!'

'Seen? I don't understand, and I didn't tell her anything...'

'Then don't! And please, *please* just keep her away from me!'

'But what did she do?'

'Nothing, as yet! She didn't get the chance, but the Athenas of this world are trouble, and...'

'Trouble? Oliver, I don't know what you're *talking* about!'

He sighed, looked momentarily exasperated. 'Paris...'

'You think I've been *gossiping*? Is that it? Having a nice girlish little chat?'

'Have you?'

'No! You think I would *advertise* it?' Her eyes wide, suddenly remembering a conversation about women who caused him trouble, she shook her head. Thoroughly bewildered, she glanced to where her sister still stood, a rather vindictive expression on her pretty face, then turned back to Oliver. 'But what did she *say*?'

'It doesn't matter,' he said dismissively. 'Just keep her away from me. More trouble I certainly do not need!'

'*I* didn't give you trouble!' she denied as though he had accused her. 'And I'm not her keeper!'

'I didn't say you were, but I would be enormously grateful if you would impress upon her that I'm a dangerous man to cross, and...'

'Are you?' she asked worriedly.

'Yes! And I do not like importuning women, of which your sister is a fully paid-up member...'

'She is not!'

He stared at her as though trying to see whether she *actually* believed that, then sighed again. 'Just keep her away from me, Paris, not only now, but in the future.'

'You're over-reacting...'

'No, Paris, I'm not. I'm issuing a warning, and if you don't want to see your sister hurt, keep her out of my orbit. And tell her to keep her pretty little mouth closed. I'll talk to you later.' A look of frustration, or was it irritation, on his strong face, he turned on his heel and walked out. Opening her mouth to call him back, she closed it again, because what on earth could she say? She didn't know what was going on!

Barely aware of anyone else in the dining-room, unaware of their curious glances, needing only to talk to Athena, she hurried after him, watched him ascend the stairs.

'Very chummy with him, aren't you?' her sister taunted scathingly from behind her.

Swinging round, wishing she understood what the hell was going on, she asked helplessly, 'What in God's name did you say to him?'

'Nothing!'

'You must have said *something*! He just accused me of... Told me to keep you away from him!'

'Well, he would, wouldn't he?' Athena said almost viciously, 'Bastard thinks he can order everyone around.'

'No, he doesn't...'

'Doesn't he? What would you call it? All I did was *greet* him, for God's sake!'

'Yes, I sa...'

'*Twice* he's done that to me! And I hope *you* haven't been daft enough to get involved with him. Not that it's very likely,' she added, her pretty face twisted with spite.

'Why isn't it?' Paris demanded, not at all flattered to be dismissed so summarily.

'A bit out of your reach, I would have thought.' With a curiously bitter smile, she added, 'I love you dearly, Paris, but even I have to admit that you're no siren. Nice,' she added moodily, 'kind, kinder than me at any rate, but you're not exactly in Oliver Darke's league, are you?'

'Aren't I? And what does that mean? That you are?'

'Me?' With a brief, unamused laugh, she said, 'Not according to him, but at least I'm not a little girl to be eaten for breakfast.'

'And I am?'

'Maybe. You can be very naïve.'

'Thank you.' Knowing that irony was wasted on her sister, and getting more and more confused by the minute, not understanding any of it, she offered quietly,

'I'm not really the innocent you seem to think, you
know.'

'Yes, you are. You *believe* people.'

'Well, that's not a bad thing, but I still don't understand why he said...'

'Leave it, Paris!' she ordered. 'Please! Just take my
advice and steer well clear of him!'

'A bit difficult to stay clear of him when I've been
interpreting for him for the past few weeks.' Amongst
other things. Things she was having trouble believing
had actually happened. 'Anyway, they're all leaving
today. Filming's finished.' But hopefully not... But what
had he *meant*?

'I know. And I was only warning you to be careful.
No need to make a production out of it.'

'*I* wasn't making the production! You were! And I'd
dearly love to know why.'

'Because I didn't want you to get hurt! You're a romantic, Paris. A fool. You don't know these people the
way I do!' she snapped impatiently.

Staring at her sister's carefully schooled expression,
remembering what Oliver had said, the way he had
looked, she began to feel just a little bit sick. 'Twice,
you said. Just how well *do* you know him, Athena?' she
asked carefully.

'Who? Oliver?'

'Of course Oliver! Stop evading the issue! You know
what I'm asking. How well do you *know* him?'

'Well enough.' Hesitating, glancing at her sister, she
shrugged. 'We met at one of those charity bashes a few
years back.'

'I see. And?'

'And what?'

'Athena! He wouldn't warn you off without reason! What happened?'

'Nothing! And why the avid interest? You aren't involved with him, you said so, so what does it matter?'

'It doesn't,' she lied, and she wasn't involved with him. Involvement implied some sort of permanency, and permanency wasn't on the agenda, she knew that. Perhaps *brief* wasn't on the agenda either... Forcing her own thoughts aside, she insisted, 'He said you were importuning... Were you? I mean, did you...?' Hating herself for this need to know, for this feeling of almost desperation that drove her, she asked quietly, 'Did you just flirt with him, or...?'

'Don't be stupid, Paris! How long have you known me? All my life! And if I want someone, then...' A rather calculating look on her pretty face, and staring in the direction Oliver had taken, she murmured almost viciously, 'And he'll pay for that.'

'Pay for what?'

'How *dare* he? I...'

'Athena!'

'What?'

'*What* happened?'

'What do you think happened?' she asked dismissively. 'We had an affair, of course. All right? Is that what you wanted to know?'

Feeling cold, feeling sick, as though all the air had been sucked out of her, she whispered, 'An affair?'

'Yes. Why not? Men *like* me!'

'He wasn't liking you just now...'

'No, he wasn't, was he?' she asked with a rather nasty smile. 'And he'll *definitely* pay for that little mistake. I know a lot of people in the film world, and he's not so great he can't be brought down.'

Horrified, and feeling even more sick, she whispered, 'Oh, Athena.'

'What? Don't be so damned *nice*. He deserves everything he gets. There was absolutely no need to talk to me as though...'

'As though what?'

'Nothing!'

Unable to leave it alone, needing to know, she asked, 'When did you have this affair?'

'Not long ago. I was feeling unloved at the time, unwanted; you know how it is.'

No, she didn't. 'And?'

'And what?'

'Don't play games, Athena! How long did it last?'

'It didn't. It was as brief as it was electric!' she taunted as she turned away. Paris turned her back.

'How long ago?'

'Oh, for goodness' sake! Does it matter? I have to go!'

'Yes, it does! How long ago?' she insisted.

'I told you! A few years! Two, if you must know,' she muttered.

'Two years?' she echoed in disbelief. 'But you were married to Chris!'

'So? There's no need to look so damned horrified! We were going through a bad patch. It happens all the time!'

Did it? Yes, she supposed it did, she thought drearily. 'Does Chris know?' Perhaps that accounted for his behaviour...

'Well, of course he doesn't! And you're not to tell him!'

'No,' she agreed listlessly. Not that she would have done. 'So why was he being nasty? Why...?'

'Was he warning me off? Because he doesn't like his "victims" to kiss and tell, of course.'

'And you were intending to?' she asked painfully. And kiss and tell who? Herself? Because he didn't want Paris to know that... Because he hoped that Athena would be discreet enough not to tell her, and her sister had refused to promise? That would account for his anger, wouldn't it? Discomfited at being confronted by his former lover, afraid she would find out, he'd got in first with a tale of her sister being... Then why had he thought she'd told Athena about *them*? And *seen*, he'd said. Athena had seen him. Where? When?

Suddenly realising that her sister had gone, she hurried after her. Distracted, confused, hurt, so very *angry*, wanting to go and accuse him, hit him, she hurried after her sister. And was that why Athena was in such an all-fired rush? In case Oliver reappeared? Afraid he would somehow punish her for her indiscretion... 'Athena!' she called frustratedly. 'Who were you intending to tell?'

'I haven't decided!' Not slackening her pace, she called back, 'I can't stop! I don't want to miss my flight.'

'No,' Paris agreed hollowly. The probably expensive flight. She was feeling bitterly used, wondering whether she was likely to see her sister's name plastered all over the tabloids, like that other girl—or was that the point? Any publicity was good publicity, and if she wanted to break into films, make her name... Oh, God. Quickly catching up with her, she asked, 'So who *is* paying?'

'Mmm?'

'And don't give me that innocent, wide-eyed look, Athena. Who's paying? Me?'

'Oh, don't be so picky, Paris! I'll pay you back!' Reaching the foyer, she turned to give her sister a quick hug, then dragged open the heavy glass door, halted, groped awkwardly in her trouser pocket, and thrust a small green card at her. 'I'll ring,' she added hastily. 'Maybe you can come out for Christmas or something. Bye. Take care.' Rushing out, she left Paris to stare distractedly down at the small credit card, and the horror she should have felt at her sister's actions didn't materialise.

'Athena!' she shouted urgently. Hurrying after her, she grabbed her arm, then didn't know what to say. 'Did you really have an affair with him?' It was almost a plea for denial.

'Oh, for goodness' sake! Does it really matter? Now?' Throwing a quick glance over Paris's shoulder, she muttered urgently, 'I have to *go*!' Climbing quickly into the back of the waiting car, she shut the door.

Feeling blank, stupid, sick, she watched the hire-car pull away. Her sister waved. She didn't in the least feel like waving back. Both sisters? And had he known? When he'd made love to her last night? Yes, of course he had. *That* was why he'd been reluctant. And did he find it amusing? Both sisters? Aware that she still held the credit card, she thrust it into her pocket with an almost frightened little movement as though it might, without her knowledge or assent, suddenly run up more bills, and turned to go back inside. She felt cold.

Oh, you fool, Paris, you stupid, stupid fool, she castigated herself as she blindly crossed the foyer. And yet, if he'd made Athena feel as he'd made her feel; dear God, don't make *excuses* for him! But why in God's name hadn't he *said* that he knew her sister? Then none of this would have happened! And even if he'd forgotten her, hadn't actually known in the beginning that they were sisters, he could have *apologised*, couldn't he? Instead of rubbishing her sister's morals? And had he whispered to Athena those words he had whispered to

her? Kissed her as he had kissed her? Made love...
Shutting her eyes tight, she drew a deep ragged breath
into her lungs, gripped the banister hard. Had he
muddled the sisters up? Had he for one brief moment
thought she was Athena? Was that why he'd hesitated?
Not because he was a famous film star and he didn't
make love to nobodies, but because he'd suddenly
realised she was Athena's sister?

And now he was up there somewhere, waiting? And
she couldn't leave, because she hadn't packed, and her
passport was in her room... Opening her eyes, she stared
upward, then gave a distressed little gasp, because he
was standing just three steps above her. Waiting. *That*
was why Athena had fled so precipitately. She'd seen
him standing there.

Tired of running away, tired of hurting, her face grimly
determined, she began to climb the stairs. Walked past
him.

'Paris!'

Head down, she ignored him, climbed on.

'Paris!' His face as set as her own, he grabbed her
arm, swung her to face him. 'What did she say?'

'Nothing! And take your hand off my arm! You
knew!' she accused tearfully. 'You bloody knew!'

'Knew? Knew what?' he asked blankly.

'Knew!' she shouted. Twisting away, she hurried up
the remaining stairs and along the corridor to her room.
Fumbling the key in the lock, she pushed inside and shut
the door.

So casual, friendly... *loving*! And then, this morning,
laughing, teasing... And yet, if it hadn't been her sister,
it wouldn't have mattered, would it? Yes, yes, it would,
but it wouldn't have been *personal*. And if she asked
him, would he deny it? Make excuses? He might not

even *have* an excuse! Might even think she wouldn't *mind*! Well she *did* mind! And she sure as hell wasn't waiting around for a discussion on it! Marching across the room, so angry, hurt, bewildered, she yanked on the wardrobe door. She would pack, get the hell out of here, go home, to sanity, safety, to a world where actors didn't intrude and mess up your life!

'Oh, *open*, will you!' she gritted. Tugging ineffectually on the stuck wardrobe door, she aimed a kick at the half-stripped panels, didn't hear the bedroom door open behind her.

'What in God's name is going on?' he demanded.

Stiffening, refusing to look at him, she continued to tug on the door. 'I can't get this *bloody* door open!'

'*Why* do you want to get it open?' he asked with a bewilderment that made her want to physically attack him.

'To pack, of course!'

'And packing makes you bad-tempered?'

'No!' she yelled. 'Being made a fool of does that!'

'Paris,' he began, 'I didn't make a fool of you...'

'No!' she yelled. 'I did that all my myself, didn't I?'

'Paris...'

'Don't Paris me! *Both* sisters!' she swung round to accuse. 'And you *knew*!'

He looked blank. 'I beg your pardon? I admit I was out of order accusing your sister, but I was...'

'Accusing?' she shouted. 'Accusing? And did you really think your little manoeuvre would work?' she demanded. 'Did you really think my sister wouldn't tell me?'

There was a little silence, a rather nasty little silence. 'Tell you what?' he asked quietly. Turning her round, he held her shoulders, looked down into her stormy face. 'Tell you what?'

'Don't touch me!' she snapped, shrugging out of his hold. 'I don't take my sister's cast-offs!'

His eyes narrowed.

'And pretending she was importuning!' she practically screamed. 'Telling her to lie makes it ten times worse!'

CHAPTER SIX

His face still blank, hands shoved negligently into the pockets of his jeans, shoulder resting against the wardrobe, he asked incredulously, 'Are you actually accusing me of having had an affair with your sister?'

'Yes.'

'And are you also accusing me of having *known* she was your sister?'

'Yes.'

'And when was this *supposed* affair *supposed* to have taken place?'

'It isn't *supposed*! And how the hell should I know when it took place? I wasn't damned well there, was I?' In the face of his continuing silence, she added angrily, 'Two years ago. And *that* was why you broke off our— the... said you had to go, because you suddenly realised what you were *doing*, didn't you? Because you still had some shred of ethics left and realised it wouldn't be quite the thing to seduce *both* sisters.'

'Is it?'

'Yes.'

'Seduce?' he asked softly.

'Yes!'

'You do hold me in contempt, don't you?' he drawled, and the brown eyes that could look so sleepy didn't look sleepy at all. 'And I thought we'd agreed, earlier, that it was *you* who seduced me. Because you were drunk.'

'Shut up! And did you ask *her* if she was satisfied?' she choked. Nervous, frightened, hurting so very much

108

inside, wishing she hadn't said anything, wishing he
didn't look as though murder might be a very nice
option, she turned quickly away, began tugging frantically at the wardrobe door again.

He made a fist, helpfully thumped it above the lock,
and the door sprang obediently open.

'Thank you,' she gritted.

'My pleasure,' he said icily.

Staring blindly at the clothes hanging limply inside,
the anger that had sustained her gone, she whispered,
'*Was* it because of Athena?'

'What?' And she would never have believed that so
much ice could be injected into one simple word. So
much contempt.

Her voice thick, uneven, she repeated. 'Athena. The
way you behaved this morning.' Eyes bleak, full of so
much hurt, the dark lashes damp and spiky, knowing
she should not ask, knowing she had to, she turned to
face him. 'Is that how it was with her?'

He stiffened, went very still, and those heavy-lidded
eyes, sexy eyes, suddenly held no expression at all.
Without a word, he straightened, caught her against him,
stared grimly down into her surprised face, and kissed
her with unyielding brutality. Shoving her away, he ordered flatly, '*Now* you can make comparisons. And if
one word, one sentence, one *intimation* gets into the
Press, I will make you wish you'd never been born.'
Opening the door, remote, almost dignified, he left,
closed it quietly behind him.

'I already do,' she whispered. There was a hard lump
in her chest, a thickness in her throat. Tears trembled
on her lashes, and were hastily wiped away. She heard
his footsteps retreat down the corridor, then silence.
Don't think, Paris. Just don't think about it. Snatching

her hands away from her mouth, where they had wandered without her knowledge, and with a determination
she hadn't known she possessed, she dragged out her
suitcase and quickly packed. Collecting her toilet things
from the bathroom like an automaton, she shoved them
all in. Such a fool, she told herself. Such a very silly
fool. And she still wanted him. The Oliver of yesterday.
And Oliver was out of her league. Had always been out
of her league.

She'd been all right until she met him, happy, contented, philosophical, and now look at her. Behaving in
a way that was totally foreign to her nature. And now
he would hate her more, because he thought she and
Athena had been conspiring against him. The way she
should hate him, for using her. And because she had
reminded him that he had once used her sister in a similar
way. Or her sister had used him. It didn't matter which,
really, did it? Only that it had happened. And it was all
so silly, because she didn't want an actor, anyway. And
he certainly didn't want her.

With a big, painful sigh, not knowing what she
thought any more, not knowing what the truth of any
of it was, she glanced emptily round, tried to make sure
she hadn't forgotten anything, and, with her scattered
emotions only barely in control, she picked up her case
and handbag and walked down to the front desk. Her
bill had already been paid, by George, the receptionist
told her with a smile. He'd left about an hour ago, and
left Paris a note. Handing it across, the receptionist
added that the others had also left. Paris was the last.
Appropriate, she supposed. All her life, she'd come last.
Shut up, Paris, self-pity is disgusting, and infinitely
boring. Neither was it true. Collecting her boots and mac,

she thanked the girl for all she'd done, and went out to her car.

It hurt, it was difficult, but it was dumb. It was also over. She could go home, try to forget him. And if George sent an invitation for a private viewing of the film... Remembering the note, she unfolded it. Just a few lines to thank her once again and wish her well, saying that he would recommend her to others, use her himself if the need arose. Hoping very much that the need wouldn't, she switched on the engine, pulled out of the car park and headed for the airport.

The same weather that had blanketed Portugal still blanketed England, and, feeling unutterably depressed, a little bit fragile, a little bit airsick from the turbulent flight, she caught the train to Victoria, and then got a cab to her flat in South Kensington. Feeling tired, slightly jaded, she gave her parked car a critical glance, saw no dents, mentally apologised to her sister who'd been using it for even expecting that there might have been, humped her case up the three front steps, and found Oliver waiting there. Staring at him in shock, she demanded raggedly, 'What are you doing here?'

'Waiting for you,' he said grimly. Grabbing her case from her lax hand, he demanded even more grimly, 'Keys?'

Too surprised to resist, she handed them over.

He opened the door, dumped her case in the hall, and waited with almost derisive patience for her to enter, then closed the door behind her.

'I don't *want* you here,' she exclaimed despairingly.

'Tough. We have to talk.'

'No, we *don't*!' Fighting for control, composure, she briefly closed her eyes, opened them and forced herself to actually look at him. At his shockingly handsome, set face. Determination gritted his strong jaw, a militant light slitted his eyes, and she desperately fought to summon up her initial dislike, squash all awareness, memory. 'Very well,' she agreed rigidly in the face of obduracy that she had no way of moving. 'What is it that I can do for you?'

'Stop behaving like a social hostess for a start. Which way's the lounge? Through here?' Without waiting for an answer, he walked along the hall and opened the door at the end. The kitchen. 'This'll do.'

'No, it won't! I don't want you here, Oliver!' Angry, frustrated, desperate to be alone, she strode after him. 'Which part are we playing now?' she asked bitterly.

'Shut up, Paris. Just shut up!'

'No! We said all that had to be said in Espinho!'

'*You* said all you had to say in Espinho,' he corrected flatly, 'and now I want clarification! You seemed to be labouring under some——'

'I wasn't labouring under anything!' she denied agitatedly. 'You don't want me! I don't want you! In which case there's nothing more to be said!'

'There's a great deal to be sai—— Ignore it,' he ordered as the telephone shrilled and she turned to automatically answer it.

'No.' Returning to the hall, she snatched up the receiver, listened, turned stiffly to look at him. 'It's for you.'

His face even grimmer, he snatched it out of her hand, barked at the unfortunate Henry on the other end. 'Damn!' he exploded. 'All right, all right...' Letting out a bitter sigh, he replaced the receiver. 'I have to go.'

Good, hung unsaid above her.

'But I'll be back,' he promised with a forbidding smile that owed absolutely nothing to humour or friendliness. She had thought she'd seen him in all his moods, whether acted or not—she hadn't seen this one, nor ever wanted to again. He snatched open the front door and left, slamming it behind him.

All the nervous energy draining out of her, she slumped against the wall, wished there were a magic carpet to spirit her away forever out of his orbit, determined that if he did return, she would never be in—and had no way of knowing how prophetic that wish might be. Feeling drained, almost ill, she shrugged out of her coat, tossed it across her case, and went to switch the central heating on. She felt very cold. A hollow, horrible feeling inside, she walked into the lounge, shoved her hands into her skirt pocket, and discovered the credit card that Athena had thrust at her. Staring down at it in renewed despair, she tossed it on to the mantelshelf. Would it never end? This nightmare? And the Green Card had to be paid off in full, didn't it? They had no credit facility like the others. How much? she wondered fearfully. A thousand pounds? Two thousand? Oh, no, not that much, please, please, not that much. And it wasn't fair, it really wasn't fair. When was it to be her turn for the cherry? Never?

Staring round her at her lovely lounge, at the pot plant that had been moved, at the photo of Athena and Chris that had been prominently displayed on the cabinet, she wanted to weep. She loved this flat: large, airy, a wide entrance hall; two bedrooms, one *en suite*; a large kitchen and bathroom; French doors on to a small terrace; she'd scraped and saved to be able to afford it after she'd left Rupert, and now it all seemed spoilt. Might even have to give it up. Might, she tried to reassure herself. Maybe she was panicking unnecessarily; maybe Athena hadn't used her card to pay for her flight... Maybe. And in the forefront of her mind, on top of the debts, the mess Athena had left, was that whispering little voice that said 'both sisters', over and over again.

What had he wanted? Why had he come? To explain? But she didn't want him to explain. Didn't want anything any more. And if the phone hadn't rung? She must remember to thank Henry if she ever saw him again, for saving her. Moving a pile of glossy magazines off the sofa, she sat down, stared blankly before her. Good old Paris, there to be trodden on, picked up and dropped like an old shoe. There to be used. All your own fault, Paris. Yes. Hardly a comforting thought. And how in God's name was she to pay everything off? And then there would be the phone bill, because no matter how hard she tried, she couldn't persuade herself that Athena wouldn't have rung the States. More than once, probably. And Athena didn't keep conversations short, did she? Especially if it wasn't her own telephone she was using. No. The only things she kept short were conversations with her sister. And the affair with Oliver. Brief, but electric.

A flash of anguish on her plain face, she tried to dismiss it, and couldn't. With a despairing little cry, she buried her face in her hands, gave in to her misery and cried as though her heart might really break.

And, over the next few weeks, with the stubbornness and determination that coloured her life, she pulled herself together, wiped away wasted tears, took every job that came along—not only in an effort to clear her debts, but to clear her mind of Oliver. She told no one about her troubles, just quietly tried to sort it all out, although it was extraordinarily hard to disguise the nervous tension, the worry.

And Oliver did not come.

December brought no let-up. Bills continued to accumulate at a frightening rate, and by the middle of the month, working all the hours she could fit in, she felt wrung out, drained. Not only was she working for the agency, but taking on any private commissions that came along. Good interpreters were always in demand, especially with so many foreign businesses starting up in Europe, English businesses getting a foothold abroad, and, although she was managing to pay her mortgage, her day-to-day expenses, she knew she would only be able to pay off the interest charges on her credit cards when those bills came home to roost, not tackle the larger amounts. And soon there would be Christmas presents to buy; she'd already had a Christmas card from Athena and Chris, but nothing else, and Christmas cards, no matter how delightful, didn't pay bills. And then the telephone bill arrived, which, as she'd suspected it would be, was astronomical. Not only had Athena rung the States, but Chris had rung her, reversing the charges.

Staring down at it, almost in disbelief, she wanted to scream. She'd lost weight, weight she could ill afford to lose. She'd had a crashing headache for the past week which no amount of aspirins seemed to shift—and her period was late. Frightened, worried, she wished she could retreat to her bed, drag the covers over her head and wait for it all to go away—only of course she couldn't, because it wouldn't. Shoving the bill on to the hall table, she shrugged into her coat, and left.

Returning home late, because the business meeting for which she'd been translating had gone on longer than expected, she stumbled wearily out of the cab they'd paid for, and wondered if she actually had the strength to climb the three steps to her front door. The pain, which had centred over her left eye, was nigh on unbearable, and she was forced to keep that eye closed in an effort to minimise it. Reaching the railing that fronted the little gardens, she rested there for a moment, groped for her key, kept her breathing shallow, because even breathing hurt, and only then became aware of the dark shadow that stood before her front door. A man.

He moved, began to descend the steps towards her, and, fighting to keep her wits about her, keep the pain at bay for just a little bit longer, she slowly straightened, gripped her keys tight in her hand.

CHAPTER SEVEN

'PARIS?' Oliver queried almost disbelievingly. 'What in heaven's name are you doing? I thought it was a drunk!'

Drunk? Yes, oh, how she wished. Allowing her tired body to slump, she just stared at him, too shocked to care that he had eventually come, then winced and held her hand across her left eye.

'Are you ill?' Reaching her, allowing the glow from the porch-light to spill across her, he hesitantly touched her arm, then exclaimed, 'Dear God, Paris, you look terrible.'

'Thank you,' she whispered weakly. 'And what on earth are you doing here?'

'Waiting for you, of course! Where on earth have you been? I ring the agency, you aren't there! You never answer your damned phone, your front door...'

'I've been busy...'

'I can *see* that,' he grated angrily. 'For God's sake, woman...' Breaking off, he removed her keys from her hand, put one arm round her and helped her up towards her front door.

'Don't put the light on,' she whispered urgently.

He made a little sound in the back of his throat, carefully negotiated the dark hall, and helped her into the room on the left, the lounge. Easing her down into the armchair, he returned to put the hall light on, so that at least he could see what he was doing, and then moved back to stand in front of her, stare down at her wan face. 'What on earth have you been doing to yourself?'

With a frown, he stepped closer, bent to tilt up her chin, refused to allow her to shrug away, and stared down into her tired face. 'Oh, Paris...'

Blanking it out, blanking everything out, keeping her eyes closed, and, so long as she didn't look at him, notice his appearance, the way he was dressed, his expression, she thought she might cope. Just. No, no she didn't, she didn't think she could cope at all. His finger burned, and she wanted to rest her head against that strong chest, be held, comforted...

'What's wrong?' he asked gently, a gentleness that was nearly her undoing. She'd managed to push him to the back of her mind, persuade herself that she wouldn't see him any more, wouldn't be affected by him any more, and now here he was, unsettling her all over again. And her head hurt *so* much, a pain that was beginning to frighten her. Each day it seemed worse.

'Headache,' she mumbled. 'It's nothing. There's some pain-killers in the bathroom cabinet.'

He went to get them, returned moments later and handed her a glass with the two tablets dissolving in a small amount of water. 'I'll make you a cup of tea.'

'Yes,' she agreed gratefully.

Slumped in the chair, too exhausted to move, in too much pain to move, she slowly drank the gritty mixture. She was aware of Oliver returning, but it took too much effort to try and open her eyes.

'You don't have any milk,' he exclaimed, sounding almost as despairing as she felt. 'Don't have any anything! The fridge is empty, the cupboards...'

'I haven't had time to do any shopping.'

'You have to *eat*, dammit! Is there anywhere open this time of night?'

'I don't think so,' she said uninterestedly, 'the garage, maybe.'

'I'll go and see.'

'You don't need...' she began, and then didn't bother. Oliver would obviously do what Oliver wanted to do. She heard the front door open and close, heard his steps on the path, and, the empty glass still held loosely in her hands, she gave in to the pain and tiredness that washed over her.

Minutes later, he was back, a bottle held in his large hands. 'Some people were just going in a few doors down, I borrowed some from them.'

'Yes,' she agreed listlessly, and momentarily wondered at the astonishment they must have felt at seeing the famous Oliver Darke on the borrow for milk. 'Thank you.' Unable to continue, because even the slight movement of her mouth in order to speak made the pain worse, she was so very grateful when he put the bottle down, carefully lifted her and carried her into her bedroom. Easing off her coat and shoes, he laid her down, pulled the duvet across her, and said quietly, 'I'll go and make your tea, and then I'm going to call the doctor.'

'There's no need...'

'There's every need.'

Whether she blacked out or just went to sleep, she didn't know, but the next thing she knew, a tall, grey-haired man was just putting his stethoscope into his black bag, his examination obviously finished. When he saw she was awake, he smiled at her, patted her hand in a fatherly fashion, got out a pen light, perched on the edge of the bed and shone it carefully into each eye. He then touched his fingers gently to each socket, her temples, the back of her neck, and sat back.

'What happened?'

She explained haltingly about the pain behind her eyes, the tiredness, and then, somehow he had got out of her all the extra work she had been doing, about not having the time or the energy to eat properly, and he gave her a look of reproof.

'Not very clever, Miss Colby.'

'No.' But unavoidable.

'Been worrying?'

'Yes,' she admitted. She didn't admit to being late, to not coming on that month. Another worry, but it might be related to the pressure she'd been under, mightn't it? Yes. It didn't necessarily mean that she was pregnant. Shoving the thought away where she kept shoving it, she waited.

He nodded, put his torch away, and got to his feet. 'Nothing radically wrong,' he assured her; 'it's called stress. Stop worrying, eat properly, get a decent night's sleep, and you'll be fine. Don't do it, and you won't,' he warned. 'The body can only take so much abuse, and then it rebels. I'll leave you some tablets, but if the pain persists, get Oliver to ring me.'

Opening her mouth to tell him that Oliver would not be there to ring, she didn't get the chance as with a last smile, he went quietly out. She heard the low mumble of voices outside her door, and then, a few minutes later, Oliver came in carrying a glass of water and a bottle of tablets. He perched on the side of the bed where the doctor had sat, stared at her, and then said quietly, reprovingly, 'You frightened me half to death.'

'I'm sorry.'

'So you should be. Here, you're to take two of these.' Shaking a couple into his palm, he handed them to her, then the glass of water. Putting a gentle hand behind her neck, he raised her, and, when she'd obediently swallowed them, he lowered her carefully back to the pillows. 'Go to sleep.' He sounded incredibly tired. Looked tired, she finally registered, and tanned. 'Sleep.'

'Oh, but...' she began worriedly.

Tucking the quilt more warmly round her, he repeated flatly, 'Sleep.' Walking quietly out, he shut the door.

Closing her eyes, she allowed a lone tear to trickle unheeded down her cheek. Oh, Oliver.

She hadn't expected to sleep, but she must have done, because, when she woke, grey light was filtering through the drawn curtains, and the pain, blessedly, was reduced to a dull ache. And then she remembered that Oliver had been here—was still here, she discovered as the bedroom door slowly opened. He glanced in, saw she was awake, and, his voice as empty as the night before, asked, 'How do you feel?'

'Much better,' she whispered. 'What time is it?'

'Half-eight.'

'Oh, Oliver, you didn't need to have come back so early.'

'I didn't, I haven't been away. I slept in your spare room. Cup of tea?'

'Please,' she agreed helplessly. Slept here? All night? And why? Because he'd been worried about her? Felt responsible? That was crazy. Before she had a chance to nag at the question further, he returned carrying one of her best bone-china cups.

'Always tastes better in fine china,' he commented as he put it carefully on the bedside table. 'Need help to sit up?' Without waiting for her to answer, he slid his arm behind her, eased her up and stacked the pillows behind her head. 'Better?'

'Yes.'

His smile was distant, mechanical almost, his behaviour unemotionally thoughtful.

Reaching out to take the cup, needing something to take her mind off him, she frowned at her sweater-clad arm. 'I'm still dressed.'

'Yes. I didn't think you would want me to...' Breaking off, he shrugged. His eyes on her downcast face, he continued quietly, 'I couldn't get back any sooner. I've been away.'

'It doesn't matter...'

'Yes, Paris, it does.'

Did it? Why? All that had happened she could lay at her own door. Not wanting a discussion on it, on anything, she murmured huskily, 'Thank you for—well, all you've done.'

'You really think I would have left you to cope on your own? Ill? In pain? Yes, I can see that you do...'

'No!' she exclaimed, then winced. 'No,' she repeated more quietly.

'Because I wouldn't do less for a dog?'

Glancing up, she sighed, gave a faint shake of her head. 'Go away, Oliver. Please.'

'Not yet.' Still watching her, he asked quietly, 'Just how much debt are you in, Paris?'

Startled, her eyes wide, she denied without thinking, 'I'm not!'

'No? Then why the need to work yourself half to death?'

'I haven't... Didn't...' Sighing, she asked, 'Who said I was in debt? William?'

'No. He wondered if you were, was worried at the amount of work you've been taking on, but didn't like to pry.'

'And you don't have the same scruples?'

'Obviously not,' he said with a bitter twist to his mouth. 'I saw your phone bill. And before you accuse me of rummaging in your private papers, it slid off the hall table, and when I picked it up... Dear God, Paris, it looks like the national debt! Dozens of phone calls to the States... Even *I* don't spend that long on transatlantic calls! Nor have people reverse the charges! Who were you ringing, for God's sake? The President?'

'Don't be silly,' she reprove weakly, 'I don't know the President. Don't know anyone in the States except...'

'Except?' he prompted.

'Nothing.'

Still watching her, he eventually asked, 'Your sister?' When she didn't answer, didn't even look at him, he continued, 'William said she'd been staying here while you were in Portugal. *She* ran up the telephone bill?'

'It's none of your business,' she mumbled.

'Isn't it? Don't you think your accusations made it my business?'

Her eyes determinedly lowered, she shook her head. She didn't *want* to talk about Athena! And certainly didn't want a discussion on on what had happened in Portugal! 'I need to get up, shower, wash my hair...'

He sighed. 'Very well,' he finally agreed, 'if you really feel up to it. What would you like for breakfast?'

Feeling defenceless and vulnerable, she just stared at him.

He stared back, then gave a small smile, a faint trace of the old Oliver, the Oliver she kept desperately telling herself she wasn't in love with. Couldn't *possibly* be in love with. 'I sent Henry out early, as soon as the shops were open, to buy provisions. He sends his love. And, before you accuse me of even more high-handedness, I also rang William, told him you wouldn't be in for a week.'

'But I have to go in!'

He shook his head. 'Breakfast. Egg and bacon? Cereal?'

'Oliver,' she protested, 'I'm very grateful for what you've done, but you can't take over my life like this!'

'I already have. Go and have your shower.' Getting to his feet, he began to walk out.

'I don't even know why you're bothering with me!'

'Don't you?' he turned to ask.

'No. I'm no one special! Not worth...'

'Expending an argument on? Well, I'd certainly go along with that.' Closing the door firmly behind him, she heard him walk along to the kitchen. Slumping weakly, she sighed. God, what a mess. And he'd looked so—distant. As though he'd been hurt. But not by her. Surely not by her. Her frown deeper, and feeling far weaker than she would have liked, couldn't actually believe, amazed at the effort it took to just shower and wash her hair, she dressed in black cords and a warm, pale blue sweater. Her energy levels almost depleted, she left her hair wet, just rubbed at it half-heartedly with a towel, then walked slowly along to the kitchen, horrified to find that she needed the support of the wall.

The radio was playing softly, a weak sun was exploring the pot-plant on the windowsill, and Oliver was fitting the teacosy over the teapot. A domestic little scene that was enacted every morning all over the country. Except that most people didn't have a famous actor playing the role of housekeeper. She wished she knew why she did. Wished she felt strong enough to cope with him, strong enough to deny the feelings. The feelings that washed over her in a wave, left her weak, tearful.

He turned, gave her a long, unsmiling look, removed
a plate from the oven and put it on the table.

'I can't eat all that!' she protested when she saw the
extent of his cooking skills Egg, bacon, fried bread,
tomato, and a sausage.

'Try.'

Sitting weakly down, more than glad to do so, she
stared at it, then at him.

'Try,' he persuaded softly. Placing a freshly brewed
cup of tea before her, he added, 'I'll leave you to eat it
in peace.'

To her very great surprise, she managed to eat most
of it, then, pushing her plate aside, she nursed her cup
before her, pondered what to do. Her brain felt woolly,
muzzy, unfocused, and, as she continued to stare into
her tea, she discovered that she didn't have a single con-
structive thought in her head. Only the knowledge that
she needed to have one. She didn't feel ill any more, just
weak. The pain behind her eyes was still there, but dull
now, only a reminder.

'Finished?'

Startled, because she hadn't heard him come in, she
nodded, pulled herself together. 'Yes, thank you. It was
nice.'

'Good. Go on into the lounge, you'll be more
comfortable.'

Opening her mouth, she closed it helplessly. It was
easier to do as he said. Collapsing into the armchair, the
armchair she had slumped in the night before, she stared
rather blankly around her, then picked up one of the
magazines Athena had left, and just stared at the cover.
This was silly.

Oliver came in, looked at her, a rather bleak light in
his eyes that she didn't see, and walked over to the

bureau. He stared down at the framed photograph that stood there, then picked it up.

Watching him from the corner of her eyes, she stiffened defensively.

There was a brooding expression on his strong face as he stared down at the picture. 'That's Chris Lowery, isn't it?'

'Yes. My brother-in-law.'

'With your sister.'

'Yes.'

'Pretty girl,' he commented almost dismissively.

'Yes.'

'And whom I'd never seen in my life until we met in Portugal.' Replacing the photograph, he turned to face her.

He didn't look as though he was lying. His face was honest, open... no, it wasn't, it was grim, but not dishonest. He's an actor, Paris, looks are his stock in trade. Yes, but... 'Athena doesn't lie,' she said quietly, despairingly.

'Doesn't she?'

'No.' But she did, sometimes. When it was expedient, when she wanted to get out of doing something. But why lie in this instance? About Oliver? There was no point. 'Why would she lie?' she asked in perplexity.

'I have no idea.'

Still staring at him, she suddenly remembered something he had said. It just popped into her mind all by itself, shoved Athena and her behaviour to one side. 'I sometimes yearn.' That's what he'd said. Yearn for what? Something he hadn't got? And why say it, then? Probably he hadn't meant to say that at all. Probably he'd...

'Why are you frowning?' he asked quietly.

Blinking, she shook her head. 'Nothing.'

'Are you all right?' he asked carefully.

'What?'

'Are you all right?' he repeated.

Her bewilderment deeper, she said, 'I don't know what you mean.'

'Yes, you do. Don't be obtuse; I'm asking if everything is all right.'

Suddenly realising what he meant, she flushed, felt a moment of panic, then steadied. 'Oh. Yes.' It wasn't necessarily a lie, she *might* be all right. Probably was.

'Sure?'

'Yes,' she said firmly, determinedly. How could she tell him anything else? Well, no, actually I'm a couple of weeks late, but don't worry about it, it's not your problem. I shan't tell the story to the newspapers. 'OLIVER DARKE HAS LOVE CHILD! MOTHER DESTITUTE!' 'Yes,' she said again. 'I'm fine.' And if she wasn't? Then what? Don't think about it. Worry about it if, and when, it happens. 'Post.'

'What?'

'The post. I just heard the letter-box.'

With a look of weary resignation, he went out to get it. For the past few weeks, she'd dreaded the postman coming, dreaded what he would bring, but now, now she was grateful for the diversion, to get off a subject that had nowhere to go.

'Bills,' he commented flatly as he tossed them on to the coffee-table in front of her. The American Express envelope was on top, and pain suddenly stabbed behind her eye.

'Aren't you going to open them?'

'No. I'll do it later. When I feel stronger, more able to cope.'

He bent, reached for the top envelope.

'Oliver! No! Don't open it!' she retorted furiously.

'Too late,' he drawled softly as he began to unfold it.

'Why can't you mind your own damned business? It has nothing to do with you!' Her worried, almost frightened, eyes fixed on his face, she whispered, 'How much?'

He glanced up, stared at her, handed it across.

'Oh, God.'

'Harrods, Fortnum and Mason, American Airlines... Expensive tastes, your sister,' he commented as he bent to pick up the other two envelopes.

'They aren't all Athena's...'

'Aren't they? Funny, I could have sworn the dates were those of when you were in Portugal.'

Biting her lip, she stared down at the horrific total.

'Electricity bill,' he continued smoothly, 'quite reasonable, in the circumstances. And your petrol account from the local garage. Two amounts prior to your departure for Portugal, and seven after.' He handed them to her. 'What else has your dear sister run up for you?'

'I don't know,' she whispered.

Staring down at her, at her white face, he suddenly swore. Stalking out, he picked up the phone in the hall, angrily punched out a number.

'What are you doing?' she called after him.

'Ringing Henry.'

'Henry?' she queried, perplexed.

'I need my cheque-book.'

Cheque-book? 'No!' she suddenly shouted. Scrambling out of the chair, she hurried into the hall, was hit by a wave of dizziness, and leaned weakly against the wall. 'No,' she breathed.

He finished talking to Henry, ordering Henry, replaced the receiver, scooped her up as though she were a child, and dumped her back in the armchair. 'Stay!'

'I'm not a dog! And you are *not* to pay my bills!'

'You can pay me back when you're solvent.'

'No!'

'Don't pay me back, then! I don't give a...' Taking a deep breath, he leaned forward, placed both hands on the arms of her chair, spoke quietly, enunciated clearly, bit out each word as though it were an enemy. 'I am paying these bills. Now, how much more do you need?'

'Nothing,' she muttered with a little glare that was unbelievably hard to maintain.

'How much?'

'Nothing!' she shouted. 'I can manage by myself!'

'How? By working yourself to death? Don't be so damned stubborn! How much? I can easily afford it.'

'That isn't the point!'

'Isn't it? What is? That we're ex-lovers?'

'Don't,' she gritted. Fighting the pain, the hurt, the shame, she muttered, 'We weren't lovers.'

'No, we weren't, were we?'

Ashamed, hurting, remembering her behaviour, wondering why he sounded so bitter when she was the one who'd been... And he was too close, unnervingly close, his mouth barely six inches from her own; she could almost feel the warmth of his skin, his breath mingling with hers. Shaken, feeling trapped, claustrophobic, she taunted agitatedly, 'Makes you feel good, does it? To help out the masses? Distribute largesse to the poor? I'm not a charity case!' If he'd looked hurt, angry, disgusted, it might have been easier but he didn't, his expression didn't change at all. Ashamed, she blurted, 'Sorry. I'm sorry.' Her eyes searching his, she exclaimed tiredly, 'Oh, Oliver, don't you see? I can't take your money, borrow more. I just can't!'

'Then have it as a gift.'

'No.'

'Paris,' he said patiently, 'with or without your consent, I am paying these bills.'

Closing her eyes in defeat, she slumped back. 'Why? Why are you doing this? You don't owe me anything!' Or was it guilt? Is that why he was here? Because he felt guilty? Searching his eyes, seeing the determination there, she gave in. 'I'll pay you back.'

He nodded, straightened, gave her a look she didn't understand at all, and began to walk out. 'I'll go and wash up.'

Oh, God. 'You don't need to do the damned washing-up!'

'Have a lady that "does", do you?'

'No.'

'Then I'll do the washing-up.'

Like talking to a bloody brick wall. 'I don't have any rubber gloves!' she shouted peevishly, then caught her breath on a sob.

Five minutes later, the doorbell rang, and she heard Oliver walk along to answer it. A few minutes later he came into the lounge carrying a bouquet of flowers. 'From William and the girls at the agency.'

'How do you know?' she demanded, aggrieved.

'I read the card,' he informed her blandly.

'Stick your oar into everything, do you?'

'Yes. Excuse me, there's the bell again. We *are* busy this morning, aren't we?'

Gritting her teeth together, she slumped tiredly, gave a despairing snort of laughter, and stared at the flowers.

Hearing the front door close, she glanced up and stared at Henry as he walked in. He, too, was carrying flowers.

'Feeling better?' he asked kindly.

'Yes, thank you.' Making an effort, another one, she managed a smile. 'Thank you for doing the shopping and everything...'

'Everything?' he teased.

'You know what I mean, and thank you for the flowers,' she murmured as he laid them in her lap. 'They're lovely.' Then she spoilt it all by adding waspishly, 'You'd better ask Oliver if I have any vases.'

He laughed and carried both lots of flowers out to the kitchen. Moments later he returned, his face unnaturally solemn. 'Oliver says you have two which he thinks will be suitable. He also says that if you get any more and you wish to use the crystal vase, to make sure you put a bit of bleach into the water, or else the glass will stain. It won't hurt the flowers.'

'Oh, good.' Fighting the inevitable, she stared at him, felt her lips twitch, and gave in. 'Oh, Henry.'

'That's better,' he praised. 'Been feeling wretched?'

'Yes,' she admitted.

'Now, where are these bills that have to be paid? I can be writing them out while Oliver arranges your flowers. And don't be embarrassed,' he added gently, 'we all have troubles in our lives. Just have to help each other out a bit, don't we?'

Her eyes filling up, her throat blocking, she searched for a hanky. 'Yes,' she agreed thickly. 'I don't deserve...'

'Yes, you do,' he said positively. Picking up the bills from the coffee-table, he retreated to her small desk with the briefcase he was carrying, and sat to begin filling in the cheques.

Blowing her nose hard, she watched him, then switched her gaze to Oliver as he came in carrying both vases, which he then arranged to his satisfaction. One on the end of the mantelpiece, and one on the bureau. The photograph was firmly relegated to the bookshelf—where it had been originally, before Athena came to stay.

'Fairy godmothers come in different guises, don't they?' she observed huskily.

Oliver turned, and his grim expression finally relaxed. 'Yes, they do. Feeling better? Like a cup of tea?'

Not knowing what else to do, she nodded.

When he returned, with tea for them all, all nicely laid out on a tray, with tray-cloth, she managed another smile. 'Your mother brought you up properly, I see. Did she like the scarf?'

He nodded, his face unnaturally solemn. 'Yes. She also said,' he added with humorous self-mockery, 'what a good job I didn't buy her the green one.'

Her smile wider, appreciative, the sparkle back in her eyes, their differences for the moment forgotten, she asked, 'Did you give it to your sister?'

He shook his head. 'I didn't dare. I'll give it to Henry for Christmas, brighten him up a bit.' Walking across to him, he bent to sign the cheques.

Watching him, so very aware of him, of his masculinity, his strength, the way he moved, looked, she only half-listened as he began to rifle quickly through the papers Henry had brought in the briefcase. He sounded authoritative, businesslike, a different Oliver, but then, she knew so very little about him, what his life was like away from the film world.

He glanced at her, smiled. 'Sorry about this—some things I need to go through.'

'It's all right,' she said softly, embarrassed to have been caught staring.

Minutes later, with a few last instructions to Henry, he turned back to her. 'I have to go out for a bit, a voice-over to redo; Henry will stay to keep you company, get you some lunch...'

'Oh, I don't need...' she began.

'Yes, you do. Don't argue.'

When he'd gone, and she'd eaten the lunch that had been cooked for her, he rang to speak to Henry.

'You're looking thoughtful,' she murmured when he returned to the lounge. 'Is something wrong?'

'Mm? Oh, no, no more than usual.'

'What does that mean?'

He gave her a faint smile and, not answering her directly, he said quietly, 'I'm glad you and Oliver have sorted out your differences.'

She opened her mouth to tell him that they hadn't sorted out anything, but he continued before she could do so, 'He's been having a rough time of it lately.'

Diverted, she frowned. 'Has he? In what way?'

'Oh, filming to finish, travel,' he mumbled vaguely. 'Then another bitch accusing him of seducing and then dumping her. Threatening to go to the Press.'

With a little jolt, her throat dry, she stared at him in shock. 'Another?' Dear God, not Athena, surely not Athena. Surely her sister's words had only been that— words, not real threats.

'Yes. Don't look at me like that,' he reproved. 'It isn't true!'

'Isn't it?'

'Of course it isn't!' he denied angrily.

'Never?' she asked quietly. 'Even that article in the papers last year? About a girl...'

'Lies!' he snapped. 'Half-truths! Innuendo! Oliver is scrupulously honest in his dealings with people. He has to be, he's a public figure—and at the least provocation,' he continued disgustedly, 'all *sorts* of dirt gets thrown at him. Death threats...'

'Death threats?' she whispered in horror.

'Yes. Rubbished by reporters...'

'Then why doesn't he sue? That girl, if it wasn't true; he didn't ever deny it...'

'To what point?' he demanded. 'Make more of a meal of it than there was? His friends, the studio, know he doesn't behave like that, and that's all that matters to him. And he tries so damned *hard* to protect his reputation, the reputation of his friends. He has to!' he added insistently as though she might be about to deny it. 'And I have *never* known him to be less than admirable.'

'Are you saying that he never has affairs with women?'

'No, I'm saying that he's always discreet, always careful.'

'And the women don't normally kiss and tell?'

'*Never* kiss and tell. Would *you*?'

'No, but then we aren't talking about me.'

'But we might have been, mightn't we?' he asked gently.

Shocked, she just stared at him. Did he *know*?

Turning away as though he did indeed know and wanted to spare her feelings, he stared from the window, sighed. 'You've never seen him as he really is,' he continued quietly, his back to her, 'not as I and a few friends know him, the *real* Oliver. This past year, he's had a really punishing schedule—filming, public appearances, charity work, trying not to let people down, and he's tired, needs a long break. I know people think that being a film star is wonderful, a piece of cake, and in some respects it is. What they don't understand, know about, are the long hours, the endless retakes, the constant travelling, living out of suitcases...'

Yes, she did; her schedule had been pretty punishing of late, and at least his paid better.

'...getting up at the crack of dawn, working a twelve-, fourteen-hour day. Sometimes more. And then there are his business interests. I know he's been irritable, short-tempered, impatient, and I know he regrets the tone he's used to you on occasion, but he's only human, Paris.' Turning back to face her, he entreated, 'Only a man. People expect so much from him, expect him to have a never-ending store of energy, goodwill. He's a generous friend, a benevolent employer. He hates lies, and he hates sham, which is possibly a contradiction in terms,' he murmured humorously, 'seeing as he makes his living doing just that, but the man you see on the screen isn't the *real* Oliver Darke. That's just illusion.'

'Yes.' Searching his thin face, she asked quietly, 'Did you know he had an affair with my sister?'

Looking slightly bewildered, he echoed, 'Your sister? Athena? The one who came out to Espinho?'

'Yes.'

His frown deepening, he shook his head. 'When?'

'A couple of years ago.'

Pursing his lips, he stared at her, then shook his head. 'Never. And I would have known,' he added, 'I've been with him five years, and *I've* never seen him with her.'

'Doesn't mean they didn't have one though, does it? Brief and electric,' she added a trifle bitterly, because the same could be said of her own—fling, couldn't it?

'Then all I can say is that it must have been bloody brief! Did you accuse him of it? Is that why he's been so bad-tempered lately?'

'Yes. No. I mean, I don't know if that's why he's been so bad-tempered. I shouldn't have thought so.'

'Shouldn't you?' he asked with an odd smile. 'And did he admit it?'

'No.'

'Then take my word for it, he didn't,' he said positively. 'He wouldn't lie to you, Paris.'

'Wouldn't he?'

'No.' Changing the subject, he asked, 'Right, what needs doing? Housework?'

'No,' she denied, 'don't be silly.' Forcing confused thoughts aside, she gave him a helpless look.

'Washing?'

She shook her head, and a little smile flickered in her eyes. 'I don't in the least understand why you're being so kind to me, you know.'

'Don't you? Because we like you perhaps?'

Yes, but *why* do you like me? she wanted to ask. But she couldn't do that, could she? Because that would sound like fishing. It was all very odd and disturbing. Unless they'd somehow discovered that she might be pregnant . . . No, surely not. Or had the doctor noticed something and told Oliver? No, that was ridiculous . . . 'What?' she asked with a frown. 'Sorry, Henry, I didn't hear what you said.'

'I said,' he smiled, 'that if you don't wish me to do anything for you, shall we have a game of Scrabble?'

'Scrabble?'

He nodded, reached for the board game that was tucked on top of the bookshelf, dragged the coffee-table in front of her, and set it out. 'I haven't played this for years.'

Neither had she. She kept it because it was a game her father had enjoyed. With a bewildered little shake of her head, she chose her chips and arranged them on their tray.

'George's film was accepted, did you hear?' he asked when they'd become thoroughly absorbed in the game.

'Yes, William told me. Good news. When does it go out?'

'Scheduled for the spring, I think—and that's not a proper word.'

'Yes, it is. Xylem. It's the woody part of a plant.' Brightening, she grinned at him, pointed to the dictionary that rested beside him on the floor.

He looked it up and gave her a thoughtful look. 'Not nearly so daft as you make out, are you?'

'I've *never* made out I was daft!'

'Have...' Cocking his head, he smiled. 'That sounds like Oliver, so I will hand you over into his care, and I will see you tomorrow.'

'I'm not a parcel!'

He grinned, and walked out. She heard the brief murmur of voices in the hall, heard the front door close, and even though she kept her attention firmly fixed on the board game she knew when he came to stand in the doorway to watch her. And all that nervous tension she thought she had managed to conquer came flooding back.

'How are you feeling?'

'Fine. Much better.'

'Good. Henry look after you all right?'

'Yes.' Fumbling all the pieces back into the box, folding up the board game, she crammed on the lid, jumped up to return it to the bookcase.

'Paris?' he asked quietly, and, when she gave him a wary glance, he added thoughtfully, 'How much of a fool am I being?'

'Fool?'

'Yes.'

Not understanding, and not having anything to do with her hands now that she didn't have the board game to fiddle with, she turned on the television, absently pressed buttons, channel-hopped. 'I wouldn't have said you were a fool at all,' she murmured.

'No, neither would I, until recently.'

When he said nothing further, she turned to look at him, her face wary, and then a little nerve jumped in her throat, as he ordered softly, 'Come here.'

She swallowed hard, shook her head, and so he moved to her, gently rested his hands on her shoulders, and, his eyes never once leaving hers, asked quietly, '*Did* you say anything to Athena, about me?'

'No,' she whispered.

'No,' he echoed thoughtfully.

Her body still, poised for flight, she asked huskily, 'What did you say to *her*?'

'It's not important,' he said in the same soft voice, 'and keep still.'

'No. Look, I don't want...'

'Didn't tell her I'd be useful?'

'Useful? No. And, Oliver, please don't...'

'But you did tell her I'd be there?'

'No!'

'Didn't tell her anything?'

'No!'

'No. We've given each other a lot of grief, haven't we?'

Surprised, she drew in a quivery breath, nodded. 'And ever since I met you,' she murmured equally quietly, 'nothing, *nothing* has gone right.'

He gave a faint smile. 'Poor Paris.'

'Don't mock me, Oliver. It *hurts*, all this—hassle.'

'You think I don't know that?'

Searching his eyes that remained so steady on her own, she asked, 'Did you want an affair with me? Is that what it was all about?' And, remembering her earlier thoughts when they'd been shopping in Espinho, added bleakly, 'Was I—*chosen*?'

He looked surprised, then shook his head. 'I don't know,' he admitted, 'I genuinely don't know what it was I wanted then. I liked you, you amused me—aroused me—but an affair? I don't know.' Looking thoughtful for a moment, he explained, 'Because important relationships in the past have—soured, I'm generally cautious of any sort of commitment until I'm sure. Until I know the person better.'

'And you didn't really trust me, did you?'

'I didn't *know* you, Paris. And you didn't trust me, either, did you?'

'No,' she admitted honestly.

'And now?'

'I don't know,' she whispered. There were still so many things unanswered. Gently removing herself from his hold, because to be so close, to have him look at her so searchingly was undermining all her determination, her resistance, she turned, glanced at the television, then stiffened in surprise. 'That's you,' she accused stupidly.

'Yes.'

Not only did she have him in her flat, but on the television as well! And she didn't want him there at *all*!

CHAPTER EIGHT

'TURN it off,' he ordered quietly.

'No.' Staring at the screen, at Oliver being interviewed, feeling so very confused, she hugged her arms round herself, listened to what was being said. Oliver very rarely gave interviews, or so Henry had said. And it seemed odd, unrealistic, bizarre. He looked handsome, at ease, charming, but not the Oliver she knew, the Oliver who was standing behind her.

'Paris . . .'

'Don't talk, let me listen.'

He gave a long sigh, walked out, and she heard him go into the kitchen.

He talked intelligently, seriously, humorously as the interviewer quizzed him about the première of his new film which was due to take place early in the New Year. A comedy, a spoof Western, that was such a departure from his normal roles . . . 'Are you worried about your fans' reaction?'

'No,' Oliver said, just the faintest quirk to his delightful mouth. 'It's a very good film. Very funny. And I did not agree to come and be interviewed to talk about the film,' he reproved humorously.

Quite unrepentant, the interviewer grinned, then sobered to show that a serious subject was about to be introduced. And then, taking Paris quite by surprise, they switched from the studio to an outside broadcast film, of Africa, to harrowing pictures of starving children—and a safari-suited Oliver. She cynically tried to tell herself that it was done for publicity purposes, but knew it wasn't. He looked tired, grubby, dishevelled, genuinely so, as though he'd been touring devastated villages for days without sleep. Was that why he had looked so tired and tanned when he'd arrived on her doorstep? Because he'd just come back?

The camera zoomed in to get a shot of him kneeling beside a child, stick-thin and probably dying—and Oliver turned his face away. Because he didn't want his expression flashed round the world? An expression of grief?

Moments later, he was walking from a hut, dark glasses now hid his eyes from the curious gaze of the cameraman. And then he began to talk about his work for the famine relief agency, about what needed to be done, how it *must* be done, how the donations everyone was so generously sending must be allowed to get through. And then back to the studio.

'Devastating,' the interviewer said.

'Yes.'

'Good of you to give up your...'

'Don't be so damned stupid,' Oliver snapped. 'What's bloody good about it? Nothing. Nothing is good about it! And until governments, both ours and theirs, *do* something, arrange, agree to an air corridor, a safe passage for trucks, try to get these warring factions, terrorists, call them what you will, to actually *talk* to each other, then yet more will die. This is supposed to be the Season of Good Will... And it is,' he added more quietly. 'Ours. God willing, let it be theirs, too. Sorry,' he apologised, 'but it makes me so damned angry. And I feel so bloody useless.'

'Thank you, Oliver Darke,' the interviewer said solemnly. 'And now, on a lighter note...' Reaching forward, she switched off the set, let the sudden silence wash over her. Hearing a movement behind her, she swung round.

'I don't want to talk about it,' he said quietly.

'No.' Searching his face, his eyes, knowing there were tears in her own, she swallowed and looked down. 'Oliver...'

He stepped towards her, pulled her against him, rubbed his palms up and down her arms as though to warm her. 'I'm sorry,' he apologised quietly. 'You mistrust actors; I mistrust—everyone. Don't you think I wouldn't like to be able to behave normally with people? Without always suspecting their motives? Do you think I didn't want to trust you? And if you hadn't thrown my lovemaking back in my face...'

'I didn't,' she protested miserably.

'Didn't you? That was how it seemed. You'd fallen asleep in my arms, a smile on your face, you'd woken to confusion, and then I was rejected. My usefulness at an end.'

'No!' Resting her forehead against him, so tired, worried, she thought she'd been through every emotion that existed lately. Joy, pain, worry, anger. 'I didn't understand what was going on! All those things you said, that Athena said—I didn't know what was truth, what was fiction. And it seemed so unlikely anyway—me, and a famous actor.'

'And if I hadn't been?' he asked quietly.

'I don't know. I'd still have been confused, hurt. I didn't know what to do, say, but I wasn't *rejecting* you! I just wanted answers, the truth.'

'As did I.'

Lifting her head, she stared into his face, remembered what he'd said when they'd woken that morning. 'You thought I used you, didn't you?'

'Initially.'

'Because you've been used before?'

'Yes. People I thought were friends, people I trusted. I'm fair game, it seems. A useful source of income. And all the dirt-dishers, the sad, lonely women with fantasies, the fanatics...'

'And which category does Athena come into?' she asked quietly. 'Because that's what this is all about, isn't it? What did you say to her?'

'It was what she said to me,' he confessed sombrely. 'Bright, so sure of her charms, she called me darling, in that extravagant way that grates on my nerves, said she'd heard all about me.'

'And you assumed she'd heard all about you from me.'

'Yes, because I thought you knew that she'd seen me. Thought she'd told you.'

'Seen you?' she whispered. 'Seen you when?' But she knew. Suddenly she knew. 'From my room? That morning?'

'Yes. You didn't know?'

'No.' Moving out of his arms, feeling sad, and lost, wondering how little she really did know her sister, she asked, 'And you saw her?'

'Yes. But I didn't know who she was then. I didn't pay her much attention, was just aware that *someone* was there.'

'And then you saw her in the restaurant? Summed her up so quickly? In seconds?'

'No,' he denied. 'I'd seen her earlier, when I first went down to the restaurant, watched her ply her charms, flirt with the film crew; George, someone, said she was your sister, and I *knew* Paris, knew what sort of person she was. I also knew that I would be a target, because I'm always a target, or so it seems . . .' Raking his hair back, he sighed. 'That sounds incredibly pompous . . .'

'But you *are* famous, well-connected, wealthy.'

'Yes. So I went back to my room, came down later when I thought she might have gone, and without much hope that she wouldn't have told you she'd seen me . . .'

'But with the hope that she wouldn't have told anyone else? But to assume that I'd admitted it, gossiped . . .'

'Yes, that was crass; so, apparently, was rejecting your sister. But I wasn't in the mood for her games, being told that I could help her new career if I wanted to . . .'

Blackmail? 'No! Athena wouldn't have intimated . . .'

'Wouldn't she? I didn't have an affair with her, Paris.'

'She said it to *hurt* me?' she whispered in disbelief. Oh, Athena, that hurt so much.

'No,' he said wearily, 'I don't think the Athenas of this world ever think of consequences.'

And he sounded so tired, so weary, and, remembering the consequences Henry *had* told her about, she let it lie. Anyway, she didn't want to discuss Athena, to think about the way she had acted, but if they didn't discuss that, what did they discuss? Where did they go from here? He couldn't be saying . . .

'What would you like to do this evening? We could go out for a meal if you feel up to it . . .'

'Oh, Oliver,' she exclaimed despairingly, 'I'm not a child, you don't have to give me treats.'

He gave a faint smile. 'I know.' Glancing at his watch, he asked, 'How long will it take you to get ready? An hour? Two?'

'Oliver, I don't want, need . . . I don't know what you *want* from me!'

'Your liking, your trust. Something to build on. Something good.'

Oh, dear lord. Something to build on? And if she was pregnant? She couldn't tell him, could she? He would immediately think ... and anyway, he wasn't asking for a commitment.

'Seven-thirty? Posh frock?'

Not knowing what else to do, she nodded, and, when he'd gone, she walked slowly into her bedroom and slumped on the bed. Oh, Oliver.

At exactly seven-thirty, he rang her bell. Staring at herself in her full-length mirror, at her carefully made-up face, the long blue Jean Muir dress, sleeveless, raggedy hem, her *best* dress, she gave a sad smile, touched a hand to her tummy, prayed ... When the bell rang again, she scooped up her wrap and bag, wondered why he hadn't used her key that he still had, and went to let him in, and then just stared. In evening suit and black bow-tie, he looked—magnificent. Out of her league. 'You look nice,' she said inadequately.

He smiled. 'Thank you. So do you.'

'Why didn't you use the key?'

His smile widened. 'Because I thought ringing the bell more—appropriate.' He offered his arm, and, feeling helpless, outmanoeuvred, she closed the door behind her, accompanied him down the path to his car—no, not his car, a fancy limousine. Beginning, against her better judgement, to feel just a little bit special, a little bit excited, she settled herself in her seat, watched him walk round to climb in beside her, and then gave him a funny little smile. 'Where are we going?'

'You'll see. Feel OK? Not too tired?'

'No, I'm fine.'

'Headache gone?'

'Yes.'

He nodded, set the car in motion, drove out towards Heathrow—and then he drove back. A little frown in her eyes, she stared at the road, stared at him, and, when they reached the very familiar territory near her flat, she asked in confusion, 'Did we forget something?'

'No,' he said.

'Then why are we...? Oliver, we're back where we started!'

'Mmm.' He switched off the engine, glanced at her front door, then smiled in satisfaction when it opened, and Henry emerged. He ran lightly down the steps, opened her door and escorted her out.

'Good evening, madam. Your table is all ready.'

Madam? Table?

Turning to Oliver as he joined them on the pavement, he continued the farce. 'Good evening, sir.' Taking the car keys, he added, 'If sir will ring when he's ready, I'll have the car brought round.'

'Thank you,' Oliver murmured politely.

'You didn't tip him,' Paris said waspishly, and he laughed, urged her inside. Closing the door behind him, he escorted her into the lounge—and shock halted her on the threshold. The long table under the window, *her* table, was covered in a snowy damask cloth, silver cutlery, candles, an enormous bowl of red roses, and champagne. Soft music played.

And, in front of her, a waiter waited. He bowed.

'Good evening, Charles,' Oliver greeted, and he sounded for all the world as though he *were* in a restaurant.

'Good evening, sir, madam. May I take your wrap?' Speechless, she handed it over.

'Your table *is* all ready,' he added as he led them towards it, courteously seated Paris before turning to Oliver. 'Would sir like me to uncork the champagne?'

'Please.'

He nodded, removed the champagne from its bed of ice, wrapped his snowy napkin round the neck, and expertly removed the cork. With a smile, he poured a small amount into her glass, then did the same for Oliver and replaced the bottle in the container. 'Five minutes?'

'Five minutes will be fine.'

He bowed, withdrew.

'Close your mouth, Paris, you look extremely silly.' Picking up his glass, he silently toasted her, then smiled. 'I wanted to dine *à deux*. If we had gone to a restaurant, and if I was recognised, there would have been speculation, murmurs, possibly reporters, and I didn't want to subject you to that. I thought this would be nicer. Intimate. And no, before you ask, it was not because I didn't want to be seen with you.'

Finally finding her voice, she asked, 'But how...?'

'I own a restaurant, remember?'

'And Charles is one of your waiters?'

'Mmm.'

'And the food? We *are* going to be fed?'

'We are. Anton has taken over your kitchen.'

'I don't know what to say.'

'Then say, Thank you, Oliver, this is lovely.'

Staring at him, then at the exquisitely set table, she gave a helpless chuckle and reached for her glass. 'If my friends could see me now... Thank you,' she said softly. 'It *is* lovely.' She touched a finger to the roses that were just coming out of bud, that were arranged in *her* crystal vase, and despite the sadness, the confusion that lurked inside, her smile widened. 'I hope you reminded whoever arranged them to put a little bleach in the water.'

'I did,' he said softly, and his smile was warm, generous, utterly soul-destroying—and she thought he was breaking her heart. 'We also thought, as you haven't been very well, that the meal should be simple. I hope you approve. Smoked salmon mousse, rib of beef, baby new potatoes and asparagus——'

'We?' she queried, feeling rather overwhelmed. 'You didn't just ring up and tell them to get on with it?'

'I did not. When I'd finished the voice-over, I went round to the restaurant, and Anton and I spent the afternoon discussing it.'

'Before you even *asked* me?'

'Mm-hm.' He smiled.

'And what would have happened if I'd refused?'

'You'd have looked extremely silly sitting there in jeans and a jumper. And then we thought, fresh strawberries,' he continued as though he hadn't been interrupted.

'*Fresh* strawberries? In December?'

He grinned. 'Being famous does have *some* advantages.'

'You're *enjoying* this, aren't you?'

'Confusing you? Yes, I have to confess I am. And now, tell me all about you,' he ordered gently. 'From when you were a little girl.'

Feeling warmed, and helpless, amused, special, as each course was served and removed, their glasses topped up, she did so. Learned about him, his family, his likes, his dislikes. Learned how well-read he was, how *interesting*, and, much to her surprise, there were no awkward pauses, no searching around for something to say as they went on to argue amiably about politics, the theatre, travel; and, when the last course had been removed, coffee brought, Charles came in to have a brief word, and return the front door key.

'Thank you, Charles, I'm very grateful. The service was superb. Has Anton gone?'

'No, sir, not yet.'

He nodded, asked Paris to excuse him for a moment, and went out to have a word with the chef. Thank him presumably. Paris would have liked to thank him, too. Her eyes following his tall figure, a feeling of unreality washed over her, and then she blinked and smiled, as Charles came to pour her more coffee, make sure she had everything, before quietly retreating.

When Oliver returned, he stood beside her, smiled, held out his hand. 'Would my lady like to dance?' And his voice was husky, intimate, and that warm little pain, that wasn't a pain at all, spread inside her, warming her, exciting her.

Getting to her feet, eyes held by his, she moved into his waiting arms, rested her head on his shoulder. He clasped one hand to his chest, his other arm round her, holding her close, his mouth against her hair, and they swayed gently to the music.

'A nice evening,' he murmured.

'Yes.' A delight. More than a delight. Special, romantic, and, suddenly, she found she wanted to cry.

'I have to go away for a few days,' he added softly.

'Do you?' Was this, then, in the nature of a farewell?

'Mmm. Paris?' he prompted, and, when she raised her head, he gently touched his mouth to hers, gave a quiet, hungry groan, released her hand and held her against him, thigh to thigh, parted her mouth with sweet insistence, and, feeling drugged, unreal, she slid her arms round his neck, pressed herself against his long frame, and still they swayed to the soft music. And it felt—

erotic, each movement, each touch of their bodies, increased her own hunger, until she was trembling.

His mouth was warm, expert, utterly impossible to resist, and if this was farewell . . . He gently removed one earring, trailed his mouth to her lobe, touched his tongue to the sensitive cord in her neck, and she gave a little moan of pleasure, of desire and tangled her fingers at his nape, moved her head blindly, searching for his mouth, and, when she had found it, touched her own tongue to the corner, felt her head grow too heavy for her neck as he slowly, softly, sensuously captured it with his teeth. Eyes closed, aware of every breath he took, every separate finger pressing so gently against her back, the unbelievable warmth of their lower bodies that still moved, swayed to the music, aroused, she groaned helplessly, 'Oh, Oliver . . .'

'I know, I know,' he murmured, and his voice was thick, husky, and that aroused her more. He tasted of champagne, coffee, mint, and her body felt as though it no longer belonged to her. Mouths just touching, moving, touching, clinging, lingering, only to begin the dance all over again. His skin was so warm, smooth, and she rubbed her nose against his cheek, his jaw, unaware of the funny little sounds she was making. Sounds of loving, wanting, desire. Like a helpless reed, swayed by the wind, she clung to him, adored him—and the phone shrilled, breaking the spell, making her jump. They drew back, stared at each other, and his beautiful eyes were darker, as she suspected her own were, and her mouth felt swollen, bereft—and the phone didn't stop ringing.

'I'd better answer it,' she whispered, her eyes still locked with his.

'Yes.'

'It might be important.'

'Yes.' A little nerve jumped in his jaw, and he drew a deep breath, set her free.

Walking dazedly into the hall, she picked up the receiver. 'Yes?'

'Paris? It's Henry. I'm so sorry to disturb you, but I need to speak to Oliver.'

'Yes.' Still feeling dazed, she turned, held the receiver out to him as he followed her into the hall.

He took it, retained her hand for a moment, pressed a warm kiss to the palm, and, his sigh deeper, held the instrument to his ear. 'Yes, Henry?'

Returning to the lounge, not wanting to eavesdrop, she stared at her roses. The warmth of the room had brought them almost fully into bloom, and she bent to inhale their fragrance, a heady scent that made her for a moment dizzy. The real world could only be shut out for an instant. A few hours at most.

'Paris?'

Turning, she looked at him, imprinted on her mind the image of him. The exquisite cut of his suit, the crisp whiteness of his shirt, the thick hair, tousled from her fingers. 'You have to go?'

'Yes. I'm sorry. My flight's been brought forward; Henry will be picking me up in a few moments.'

'Back to work?'

'I'm afraid so. A meeting I'd set up in the States. You'll be all right?' He didn't approach her but remained standing in the doorway, one shoulder resting against the door-jamb.

'Yes. I'll be fine.' I love you, she told him silently. Perhaps I've always loved you—and the thought didn't shock her as it should have done, just left her feeling more and more bereft, as though the world were ending.

'Don't worry about the candlesticks, the cloth; someone will come round to pick them up tomorrow. Anton's left the kitchen tidy.'

'Yes. Thank you.' Words, lots of words, because neither of them knew how to part?

There was a toot from outside, and he jerked as though it had taken him by surprise, then gave an odd smile. 'Come and see me off.'

She nodded, forced herself into action. She felt a bit like a marionette, operated by someone else. Someone who didn't know her. At the door he halted, one hand on the latch, then turned, searched her face. 'Take care,' he murmured throatily.

'Yes. And you.' And then he was gone, and she closed the door with a hand that shook. He hadn't said he would be back. So now you must be sensible, Paris, put him out of your mind. Forget him—and find out for sure if you are pregnant. Shutting her eyes to the problem wouldn't make it go away. She had to *know* and then deal with it. So sensible, Paris—and she touched her fingers to the tears that poured so silently down her face.

CHAPTER NINE

STARING at the little strip of paper, feeling frightened and alone, Paris gave an involuntary shiver. Twice she'd done the test, and twice it had come out positive. She'd hoped against hope that she'd been wrong... Putting her hand on her tummy, tears prickling her eyes, she bit her lip in worry. How in God's name was she going to cope with a baby? The difficulties would be enormous. There would be heartache—oh, stop it, stop it! Don't be so damned selfish! What about the little one? How would the baby cope? No father... With a frightened sob, she slumped back on the couch. She couldn't tell him—he had his career, his reputation... And he wasn't intending to come back, she *knew* he wasn't, so he wouldn't find out, and...

Oh, dear God. But she'd have to go and see the doctor, be sensible—everyone at the agency had private medical insurance, arranged by William, so it would be an easy matter—and once he had confirmed it...and there wasn't anyone to share it with, to tell. She couldn't tell Athena, didn't *want* to tell Athena, and, for the first time in a very long while, she wished her parents were there. A mother to hug her, tell her it would be all right, that they would manage... Oh, Paris, you're twenty-nine, other people manage...

A few days later, the pregnancy confirmed, an appointment made at the local clinic for the middle of January, she returned to work. If she stayed at home

153

she would brood on it, on Oliver, and life had to go on. Yet everywhere she went, it was there, in the forefront of her mind. Pregnant. A baby. Oliver's baby. She wouldn't be able to work, not for a bit anyway, and, even when she could, what sort of life would it be? She couldn't seem to even *comprehend* the changes that would take place. The responsibility, the worry—the love? And if she didn't have it? The guilt... No, she couldn't even think about that. But first there was Christmas to get through, and then a job interpreting for a Madame Duchesnay in the French Alps who was having a dinner party for some English guests. She was a bit puzzled by the request, as was William, because there were any number of French interpreters she could have used, her own countrymen and women, but apparently Paris had been recommended, and she was insistent that she come. And, as William said, it would be a break, and she definitely looked as though she needed one of those.

The ferry was booked for the day after Boxing Day, because Paris had decided that she would quite like to drive down, stay overnight somewhere—and it would probably be the last chance of a holiday for some time to come. There was no word from Oliver over the Christmas break, a Christmas she was spending alone because she didn't want to talk, be festive, pretend. Not even a Christmas card. Her head told her it was best. Her heart felt broken.

Her mind and emotions still in turmoil, trying to be positive, in control, she drove down to Portsmouth to catch the overnight ferry, forced herself to consider the forthcoming dinner party, and the next morning, after a night spent tossing and turning, belatedly wondering whether morning sickness was a possibility, she set off into the French countryside. She stayed overnight at a motel on the outskirts of Bordeaux, and, by early afternoon the following day, finally reached Pau. Taking the small secondary road, as she'd been instructed, she drove upwards towards the mountains, and all during the long drive she thought about Oliver. Oliver in Africa; Oliver being kind, caring, loving; Oliver as a father. Days were passing at a frightening rate, while inside her, growing, was his child, and she felt wretched, guilty, because she was deceiving him.

Following the clear directions, she turned off again, and then began looking for the house. It was tucked between tall pines, a cross between Uncle Tom's Cabin and a Swiss chalet. It looked solid, well-built, cosy. Smoke rose lazily from the chimney, a fire fed by the gigantic log pile to one side. There was ample parking for half a dozen cars on the triangular gravelled drive. A drive that this evening would no doubt be full as guests arrived for the dinner party. A dinner party that would perhaps remind her of another one. One that had been special, a delight—a farewell.

Forcing the memories aside, climbing stiffly from the car, she stretched, shivered in the chill wind, collected her case, and went to knock on the solid wood front door. It was opened instantly by a smiling woman.

'Madame Duchesnay?'

'*Oui.*'

She held the door wide, and, as Paris stepped in, Madame Duchesnay stepped out, and closed the door behind her. How very odd. Somewhat bemused, she stared at the closed front door, carefully put down her case, and wondered what on earth to do next.

'Hello?' she called cautiously. Nothing. She could hear the snap and crackle of flames from the room a little down on her left, see the faint glow from the fire. Feeling a bit foolish, she tippy-toed towards it and peeked inside the room. No one. Oh, this was silly, and she didn't know why on earth she was tippy-toeing; she'd been *invited*, after all! Walking more normally, she entered the room, stared round her at pine-clad walls, comfortable furniture, polished wood floors with exquisite rugs scattered on them, heavy cream flecked curtains that would shut out the darkness... and then gave a little start as a hand holding a book appeared over the arm of the chair nearest her. The chair facing away from her, towards the fire. The book was placed spine up across the arm, leather-slipper-clad feet appeared, and then a tousled fair head—and her heart slid down to her stomach, then up, to block her throat.

There was joy, then anguish, as he stood, turned, gave her a long, unsmiling look.

'Oliver?' she whispered hoarsely. 'What on earth are you doing here?'

'Waiting.' He didn't look welcoming, or friendly, and he certainly didn't look *loving*; he looked unbelievably grim, and her brief anticipation flickered and died. 'Give me your coat.' An order, not a polite request.

Shrugging out of it, her eyes still fixed widely on his face, she handed it over.

'Sit down. I'll get the tea.' Taking her coat with him, he walked out.

Feeling sick and frightened, because this wasn't a reunion, a moment for hope, she put her bag on the chair arm, moved to stand by the fire, to stare down into the leaping flames. Did he know? Had he somehow found out? No, of course he hadn't, he *couldn't* have done! But what, then, was he doing here? Invited himself to the dinner party? Hearing the soft slap of his slippered feet behind her, she flicked him a glance and swallowed nervously.

'Yes,' he agreed flatly, 'you might well look frightened.' Placing the tray he carried on the coffee-table, he straightened, faced her. 'And don't turn away,' he ordered, 'I want to see your face while you lie.'

'What?' Her heart beating suffocatingly fast, she searched heavy-lidded eyes, found nothing to comfort. Latching on to incidentals, she stared at the thin black roll-neck sweater that he wore, the grey trousers... He *couldn't* have found out, she told herself frantically, no one *knew*. Yet her hand went automatically to her stomach in a protective little movement, and then she forced herself to remove it before he noticed. Her heartbeat might be erratic, her palms damp, but she must not let him see how frightened she was. How worried.

'You're a guest at the dinner party?' she asked stupidly, knowing even as she said it that it couldn't be true, that fate didn't work that way.

'No. There is no dinner party.'

No, of course there was no dinner party. 'Madame Duchesnay?'

'She lives in the village, looks after me when I'm here.'

'Here?'

'Yes.'

'This is your house?'

'Yes. Sit down.'

She sat. Not tidily, not elegantly, just collapsed downwards. His house?

'Heard from Athena?'

'What?' she asked blankly as he lowered himself to the sofa and began to pour the tea. 'Athena?'

'Yes, Athena.'

'No—well, I had a Christmas card...' Oh, my God. *That* was it! Athena had told people, the Press, as she'd threatened. 'Oliver, she wouldn't mean, she doesn't think...'

'She didn't write? Send you a cheque, as promised?'

'Pardon?' Wrenching her mind away from law-suits, publicity, she automatically took the cup he held out, stared at him in bewilderment. 'Send a cheque? Promised? Promised who? You?'

He gave an arctic little inclination of his head. His hands were clenched on his own cup, she saw, his muscles rigid.

'You've *seen* her? Talked to her?' she asked nervously. 'When? When did you see her? And *why*? How did you even know where she lived?'

'I was going to the States, I told you. And while I was there, decided to look her up. I got her address from the Christmas card she sent you. As to the *reason*, I wanted to ask her why, if she loved you, as sisters presumably do, she left you with a mountain of debts that you made yourself ill trying to pay off—and why she lied.'

'And what did she say?' she whispered.

'That she hadn't known you couldn't pay them off, that she was intending to reimburse you, that you should have *told* her. It went along the lines of "How on earth am I supposed to know things if she doesn't tell me? She *never* tells people things!" And you don't, do you?' he asked softly, and with just the faintest hint of— menace.

'Yes. No.' Nervous, frightened, almost able to believe that he might be able to *see* that she hadn't told him something, she burst out, 'I don't know, do I? And I didn't mean what did she say about the money, but about lying! *Did* she?'

'I told you she did.'

'Yes,' she agreed almost despairingly, because it didn't really matter *now*, did it? Although, she supposed it would be nice to know her reasons. 'Why? Why did she lie? Not to hurt me?'

'She lied because she's spoilt, because she likes to show off to her big sister, wants to be—important.'

'But lying about you doesn't make her important. That's just silly.'

'Silly to you. Not silly to her,' he corrected. 'What did she say? To stay away from me? That I ate little girls like you for breakfast?' One eyebrow raised, he waited.

'Yes,' she whispered. 'That she'd met you at a charity do somewhere. Said...'

'That we'd had an affair? Brief but electric?'

Horrified, she exclaimed, 'Athena would never have told you that!'

'No, Henry did. He thought I'd be interested. Which, of course, I was.' Still watching her, his face expressionless, he added softly, 'Is that why you didn't tell me?'

'Tell you?' she whispered.

'Don't play games!' he shouted, making her jump. Slamming his cup down he got to his feet, edged round the coffee-table and came to stand in front of her. 'You lied to me. I asked, specifically, and you lied. And I want to know why.'

'I don't know what you mean.' Her voice barely audible, her neck crooked at an awkward angle as she stared up at him, frightened eyes fixed widely on his face, she waited. He might not mean... What else could he mean?

'Yes, you do. How long were you intending to keep it to yourself? A week? A month? Forever?'

'I don't know what you're talking about!' she shouted.

'The baby,' he said flatly. 'My baby. Or is it?'

Oh, dear God. Playing for time, trying to think of something, *anything* to say, she put her cup in the hearth and queried shakily, 'Baby?'

'Yes. As in small child, as in—pregnant. So is it? Mine?'

'No,' she said quickly, too quickly.

'Not mine?'

'No.'

'Rupert's?' he asked with quiet savagery.

Shock replacing her fear, she queried blankly, 'What?'

'Rupert. The Rupert you walked out on without explanation, consideration.'

'The Rupert I did what to?' she whispered faintly. 'And how on earth do you know about him, anyway?'

'Athena.'

'Athena told you?'

'Yes,' he said grimly, 'and although I wouldn't normally give credence to anything she might say, in this instance she seemed to be telling the truth. Does he know?'

'Rupert?'

'Of course bloody Rupert!' Gripping her arm, hard, above the elbow, he yanked her to her feet, looked as though he wanted to shake her. 'Does he?'

Feeling as though her life was unravelling before her eyes, she weakly shook her head. 'No, of course he doesn't know. I don't even know how you know.'

He gave a mirthless smile. 'My doctor. The doctor who came to see you. The doctor who, because he was worried about you, contacted your GP, who was happy to tell him of your pregnancy...'

'That's unethical!'

'I don't care what it is!' he gritted, the soft tone gone. 'All I care is that my doctor, naturally,' he pointed out sarcastically, 'thinking I would be ecstatic, congratulated me!'

Oh, God. Slumping in his hold, she just stared helplessly at him. He looked bitter. Implacable. And those beautiful, heavy-lidded eyes hard, accusing. Feeling drained of emotion, wavering between dream and reality, she asked faintly, 'Why did Athena tell you about Rupert?'

'Because, unlike you, she's a very sharp lady.'

'I don't know what that means.'

'Don't you?'

'No. What did she say?' Might as well know it all, mightn't she?

'That he did everything for you. Adored you.'

Remembering just what sort of adoration he'd offered, she gave a humourless smile. 'Doesn't sound very likely, does it? Plain little Paris Colby being adored?'

'Shut up,' he snapped viciously. 'I'm not in the mood for games! She also said,' he continued, sounding extraordinarily vindictive, 'that, having helped you in your career, the moment he had a chance to further his own, you refused to accompany him, translate with foreign producers and walked out. Broke his heart.'

'Oh, sure, broke it so badly that he immediately jumped into bed with the producer's daughter he'd been carrying on with, and then married her.'

'I see.'

'Good.'

Refusing to be sidetracked, he asked, 'That's why you didn't tell me about the baby?'

Feeling almost hysterical, hovering between dishonesty and expedience, she nodded, what the hell else could she do? And he'd have had a bit of a shock if she *had* told him. If it had been Rupert's baby it would have been born by now. Athena had obviously not told Oliver *how* long ago they'd broken up.

The silence lengthened, became even more uncomfortable. 'Why did you sleep with me, Paris?' he asked quietly. 'To find a father for the child you were already having?'

'What? No!' Unbelievably shocked, she touched a hand to his chest, then hastily removed it as though she'd been burned. 'No! Dear God, Oliver, what sort of person do you take me for?'

'I don't know, that's why I asked.'

'You really think... And even if I had, I'd have *told* you, wouldn't I?'

'Would you? And the bills?'

'Bills?' Unable to make the connection, she just stared at him.

'Post.'

'Pardon?'

'Post,' he repeated flatly. 'I remembered, you see, how you neatly turned aside the question of Athena, angrily insisted you didn't need my help...'

'I didn't!'

He gave a mirthless smile. 'Then why tell me the post had arrived, *knowing* it was likely to contain bills?'

'Because I wanted to...'

'Distract me?' he asked softly.

'Yes... No!' And he looked so hurt, so tired, and, wishing she knew if she was doing the right thing, she put out her hand as if to touch him again, then let it drop to her side. What else was there to say? Nothing that would be any use. Aching for him, for herself, wishing he didn't look so—distant, she whispered, 'It wasn't anything to do with the bills. I *didn't* want you to pay them.'

'Any more than you didn't want me to think I was the father of your baby?'

'No. Oh, Oliver, no.' Yet wouldn't it be best for him to hate her? Go away, never come back? Her eyes full of tears, she swung away, the ache in her heart almost too big to cope with. And even if she did tell him the truth, what would that solve? Anyway, it wouldn't be fair. If he'd loved her, perhaps, but he didn't. Was fond of her maybe, *had* been fond. Why did things always get in such a muddle? she thought despairingly. When she'd left Rupert all those months ago, found her flat, she'd got her life in order. For the first time in her life that she could remember, she'd got things *straight*. A lovely place to live, a good career, friends, and she'd thought that life was beginning to be pretty damned good. Independent, solvent, happy. And then she'd done her sister a favour, then William, gone to Portugal...

So many lies, Paris. She *hated* to lie. Especially hated to lie to someone who had been kind to her, and she wished with all her heart that it could all be different. If only he didn't look like someone she could have loved. Did love. If only he could have loved her. If he hadn't been famous, so shockingly handsome, so elegantly special... Oh, stop it, Paris, stop it. You've made your bed, no use rumpling the sheets now. And it hurt. Dear God, how it hurt.

Wanting to make it easier for him, for herself, deciding it would be best to leave, find a hotel for the night, she went to grab her bag off the chair arm, and, because her vision was so blurred, she missed the strap, knocked it to the floor instead, and watched the contents spill all across the carpet—including the little white hospital appointment card. Staring at it in horror, she lunged— Oliver was quicker. Bending, he picked it up, held it out of her reach. Held it absently, his eyes fixed on her stricken face.

'I have disliked a great many people in my time,' he said with a quiet ferocity. 'Despised them, been angry and disgusted. But, until now, I have never hated.'

Closing her eyes, wanting to die, she whispered painfully, 'I'm sorry.'

'Sorry? Yes. I imagine you are. The Golden Goose is—dead.'

'No! I wanted *nothing*!'

'Didn't you? Then why are you looking so frightened? Why does it matter that I know?'

Even more frightened, she denied quickly, 'It doesn't. I'm not.'

'Aren't you? When's the baby due?'

'Due?' she echoed in horror.

'Yes, due. And just in case you are still considering lying, perhaps I should explain that Athena told me when you and—Rupert——' he enunciated as though the name tasted impossibly vile '—broke up. So, how many weeks pregnant are you?'

He waited, and when she didn't answer, he glanced at the card he held, at the heavy black wording on the front which proclaimed its use for all to see, and then returned his eyes to hers. 'Well?'

CHAPTER TEN

'GIVE me the card, Oliver,' she managed quietly.

He shook his head.

'It has nothing to do with you.'

'Then why are you so agitated?'

'I'm not. I...' Breaking off, she could only watch in helpless horror as he opened the card, glanced at it, and then he went very, very still. He stared at it for endless moments, then moved his eyes to hers. He looked dumbfounded, then anguished. 'It says nine weeks.'

She swallowed hard.

'Which makes it—mine. Doesn't it? Doesn't it?' he grated savagely.

'Yes,' she agreed thickly.

'And you're going to have it...' Closing his eyes, he crushed the card in one strong fist, dragged a breath deep into his lungs. 'Oh, dear God,' he whispered. 'Terminated.'

'What?' she queried in fright.

Opening his eyes, his face white, so very bleak, he shouted raggedly, '*Mine*! My child! And you were going to get rid of it without even bloody telling me! If I hadn't found out...'

'No! Oliver, no!' Her eyes wide, she held out her hand in helpless appeal.

'Yes!' Straightening out the card, he shoved it at her. 'Pregnancy termination! That's what it says! On the eighteenth of January...'

'No!' Grabbing the card, smoothing it out, she showed it to him again, made him read it. 'Examination! Examination!' she repeated. 'Look!' Reaching out, she hesitantly touched his hand, then flinched when he stepped back out of her reach. 'Oh, Oliver,' she whispered sadly, 'that didn't even occur to me. I wouldn't do that, *couldn't* do that... Really, I couldn't.'

'Couldn't?' he repeated savagely. 'Couldn't?' Eyes almost black, nostrils pinched, his face grey, he suddenly turned, slammed his hand violently against the wall, making her jump. Taking a deep breath, he finally looked up, raked her worried face. 'And you weren't ever going to tell me, were you?'

'No,' she whispered.

'Why? And why pretend it was Rupert's? Because you wished it were his?'

'No! Dear God, no.'

'And how the hell did you think you were going to manage?'

'Am going to manage,' she corrected quietly. Collapsing down on to the chair arm behind her, her eyes fixed on his forbidding countenance, she began again, 'Oliver, I...'

'Don't,' he gritted savagely. 'Don't tell me how bloody good you are at coping! How you had it all worked out! That I was superfluous! God,' he exploded as he lurched upright, 'do you have any idea how that makes me *feel*?' Striding across the room, and then back, he leaned towards her, his hands clenched as though to keep from striking her. 'And he—she,' he castigated, 'would have grown up never knowing that *I* was the father! And if it hadn't been for the doctor, I would never have known that I was going to *have* a child! I could *kill* you!'

'Oh, Oliver,' she exclaimed brokenly. Reaching out, she gently touched one clenched fist, stared at his anguished face. 'It wasn't a question of not wanting you to know, of trying to hide it because I didn't want you to be a part of it...'

'Want?' he demanded. 'Want? I *am* a part of it!'

'Of course you are, but how could I *tell* you?' she asked in distress. 'Just think about it for a minute. I didn't know what you wanted from me—no, don't interrupt, I didn't. An affair? Friendship? You, a famous film star, a man who could have any woman he chose...' Standing and putting her fingers over his mouth when he would have spoken, she continued, 'And who was I? No one. A little interpreter. How could I have told you? It would have looked like a trap. And if not a trap, then a plea for money.'

'And you didn't want anything from me, did you?' he asked bitterly.

'I didn't want anything you weren't prepared to give *willingly*,' she corrected. 'I...'

'And how the bloody hell could I give it willingly if you didn't damn well tell me?'

With a tired, exasperated little sigh, she grumbled, 'I didn't not tell you because I didn't want you to *know*! Because I wanted to keep you from your child! I didn't tell you because...' Hesitating over her choice of word, she resumed firmly, 'because I like you too much. Respect you too much. And stop looking at me with such an expression of pained disbelief! How would it have looked? Like blackmail, that's what! For goodness' sake! It's only a few weeks since Henry finished telling me about importuning women! How they follow you, write to you, give you grief. The girl in the papers! I didn't want to trap you!'

'Trap? Knowing how very much I wanted to be trapped?'

'What?'

Throwing her a look of disgust, he swung away and continued ranging angrily round the room. 'You think I normally play housekeeper to my women friends? Do their cooking? Pay their bills?' Coming to a halt, he turned to face her, accuse, 'You really think I would arrange that farce of a dinner party! And you knew *then*, didn't you?'

'No,' she denied, her voice almost a despairing wail. 'And it wasn't a farce, it was beautiful...'

'Beautiful!' he derided.

'It was! But I didn't think you'd be back!'

'Don't be so damned stupid! Of course I was coming back!'

Dumbfounded, she just stared at him. 'You didn't say... You left so quickly...'

'Of course I left quickly! If I hadn't left then I wouldn't have bloody gone! I don't do *any* of the things I've done for you!' With a bitter laugh, he continued, 'I hurried home, eager to tell you what your sister had said, ask you about Rupert, invite you to spend Christmas with me—and then I saw the doctor!'

'I didn't know...' she began helplessly.

'Yes, you *did*. You aren't a fool!'

'But you never explained! Haven't explained now!'

'I didn't think I needed to! God, I don't think I even know *what* to say to you any more!' Giving her a look of savage fury, he stormed out.

Long after he'd gone, the room still seemed to echo with his words, the front door echo from his slam, the faint sound of footsteps on the gravel. Feeling numb, somehow disbelieving, sick and empty, she walked across to the window, dragged back the heavy drapes, and, her arms protectively round her waist, she stared out over the dark Alps. She couldn't see very much, just an impression of jagged mountain peaks, the occasional flash of light as a car rounded a distant bend, headlights carving a momentary brilliance, only to fade and leave all as before. A few stars relieved the black of the sky, a misty moon, full. Happy New Year, Paris. Swallowing a sob, squeezing her eyes tight shut, her mouth twisting with pain, she fought for control. Felt ill.

Holding her breath for a moment, she slowly released it, watched it fog against the window. And if he'd felt as he said he'd felt—intimated how he'd felt—how could he accuse her of all those things? Believe things about Rupert, the bills... And what came next? Nothing? A financial arrangement?

She didn't really know how long she stood there staring out over the distant range, an hour maybe, perhaps longer. Her mind almost blank, her body cold despite the central heating, she let the curtain drop, walked back to the fire. The light suddenly dimmed, on a time-switch perhaps, and she knew she should go, find her coat...but the thought was hazy, without energy, and, instead of making plans, she slumped tiredly on to the sofa, stared at pictures in the fire, remembered the night he had taken her to dine. Barely a week ago, and she swallowed hard, closed her eyes, allowed the tears to fall. How special could it have been if she hadn't got pregnant? If she had been honest with him? There was no way of knowing, but still her mind continued to taunt her with visions of how it might have been. A loving couple, a baby... And nothing, nothing, could be as bad ever again, could it?

Wrapped in her own misery, she didn't hear the front door open, didn't hear the soft footsteps in the hall, only became aware of his return when a gentle hand touched her shoulder.

Jerking as though shot, she turned to stare at his shadowy form.

'I'm sorry,' he apologised, 'I didn't mean to startle you.'

Her heart still hammering, she shook her head, realised he probably couldn't see the movement in the dark room, and whispered thickly, 'It's all right.'

'Is it?' he asked gently, and then his weight was beside her, dipping the sofa cushion, strong arms held her close, drew her against his warm body, yet his cheek against her own was cold, his hands touching hers were chilled.

'I've been out walking,' he explained raggedly. 'Thinking. I'm sorry.'

Not sure her voice would work, she shook her head, and, afraid to relax against him, held herself stiff.

'What does that mean?' he breathed against her cheek. 'No talking? No apology?'

With another long sigh, she managed, 'No, I meant that you have nothing to be sorry for. I made the mess. Asked for all I got.'

'Did you?'

'Yes. I wasn't trying to hurt you...'

'I know.'

'Do you?' She didn't look at him, couldn't look at him, because she knew it would be her undoing. She had to be strong. 'Oliver...'

'No,' he said gently. Moving slightly, resting his chin on top of her head, cuddling her more warmly against his chest, trying to melt her stiffness, his arms a solid band around her, he continued, 'Don't tell me how strong

you are, how you can cope. Don't tell me that I'm rich
and famous, that no way must I be allowed to become
involved with a little interpreter. Don't tell me how it
would ruin my reputation if it became known. Just tell
me honestly, without lie, prevarication, how you feel
about me. About *me*, the man. Forget for the moment
all the worry, heartache, the baby; just tell me honestly
how you feel, how you felt before all this happened,
before my accusations. How you felt the night we—
danced. The truth.'

The truth? Would that be best? And didn't she at least
owe him that? After all the lies? And it was no good
saying she wasn't affected by him, because he would
know it wasn't true. But she could tell him it had just
been an attraction, over now...

'The truth, Paris,' he repeated softly.

With a little shiver, touching the hands that held her,
a small contact to give her courage, so unbearably aware
of the steady heartbeat against her side, the soft breaths
that fractionally moved his chest, the wishes, the hopes
that filled her, the pain, she stared into the leaping
flames, and began to tell him. Honestly. 'When I first
saw you, it was as though everything that had happened
to me before wasn't there any more. All my hopes,
values, dreams fled—to be replaced by awareness of you.
And it made me angry. Who were you, to disturb me
so? An actor, a man practised in deception, illusion. And
so I denied it, fought against it, refused to see the man
beneath. And then you kissed me—and it was as though
I'd never been kissed before.' With a little sad sigh that
contained perplexity, misery, confusion, she leaned back
into his embrace, clasped his hands tighter. 'And it was
all so silly. And then you started being nice to me, and
that wasn't fair, Oliver, because it polished the dream—

and the dream was impossible. And even if it hadn't been, I didn't want to be involved with an actor again. I'd had enough of the film world when I'd been seeing Rupert . . .'

'Seeing?' he asked carefully. 'Or living with?'

'Living with,' she confessed quietly. 'I'd met him at a party that Athena and Chris had thrown, and he seemed different, nice, not shallow and egotistical like the rest. Only that too was illusion. Perhaps I was flattered, I don't know. But he didn't adore me, Oliver, he used me—and Athena couldn't understand why I minded. He was just beginning to make a name for himself, getting offers from foreign producers; he needed me to translate. Because I was there, because I was handy, didn't make waves . . .'

'Didn't? Doesn't sound like you.'

With a faint smile, she agreed. 'No. But I thought I was in love, you see. I wasn't really happy in that world; people weren't—kind. Oh, they pretended to be, but mostly everyone had an eye to the main chance, and it didn't seem to matter who you trampled on to get to the top.'

'We're not all like that.'

'I know. But I wanted you to be like that, because then it might stop the feelings.'

'And did it?'

She shook her head. 'And then I had too much to drink—I told myself I'd had too much to drink, and that was why I behaved as I did, but it wasn't true. Not true at all—or not entirely. I wanted you, wanted your warmth, your love—not to keep, I knew I couldn't have that, and I didn't mean for it to be physical, a union— that just happened. But I didn't regret it, or not until Athena said . . .'

'She'd had an affair with me.'

'Yes. And all I could think was—both sisters. If I hadn't accused you, if I hadn't been ill—if I hadn't become pregnant. And oh, Oliver,' she exclaimed sadly, 'how could I have told you? I could tell no one. Loving you, how could I ever have told.' There, it was admitted. Love. And it *was* a release. With a faint, sad smile, knowing he was intelligent enough to understand, not to feel guilty for her idiotic behaviour, she turned her face slightly and touched her cheek to his shoulder. 'I knew, always knew, that it could go nowhere; that was why I fought so hard against my feelings. I didn't want to be hurt, and knew that I would be.'

His mouth touched her hair, his breath feathered across her face as he spoke, but not, initially, about what she had confessed. 'Your hair smells of apples and spices, warm, heady... How long were you with him?'

'Rupert? A few months.'

'And when did you leave him?'

'Last March. What did Athena say?'

He gave a humourless laugh. 'Before you went to Portugal.'

'Oh, Oliver.'

'Yes. Ambiguity. But I was angry with her, and perhaps because she saw something I didn't want her to see she tried to pay me back. She knew, or suspected, that mention of another man *would* hurt.'

Hurt? Or disappoint? 'Sharp lady,' she murmured, remembering his words.

'Yes.'

'And you recognised her for the lady she was, isn't that what you said?'

'Yes. Because she was like so many others who try to cause me grief. Because I'm well-known...'

'Famous,' she put in.

'All right, famous. Wealthy, a hot property,' he added cynically. 'But I don't like that world any more than you do, Paris. I don't go to their parties, drink with them, play with them. I do my work, and go home, or back to wherever I happen to be staying. And over the years I got a reputation for being difficult, moody, hard to work with...'

'Which doesn't bother you at all.'

'No.'

'Because you have your own good friends who know you for what you are.'

'Yes.'

'And so Athena lied.'

'Yes. And the truth of the matter is that I probably did meet her, briefly, at some charity do. She said I did anyway, expected me to remember her.'

'And you didn't. But you don't say you had an affair with someone just because they don't remember you!'

'Not most people, no. Not you, but Athena isn't like you, is she?'

'No. She's beautiful, and...'

'Paris,' he warned. 'Don't.'

'What?' she asked, puzzled.

'If you put yourself down just once more, I shall be extremely angry. And do *not* compare yourself to your sister to your detriment. You're worth a hundred of her! She's spoilt. *You* probably spoilt her. Your parents...'

'Yes,' she admitted, 'she was easy to spoil. She wasn't always hard—deceitful,' she added reluctantly. 'But when our parents died, perhaps I tried too hard to make up for their loss, pushed her into being someone she wasn't... And I wasn't putting myself down. She *is* pretty, and, I suppose, I was always proud of that. My lovely little sister.'

'Lovely on the outside,' he corrected. 'And perhaps you all gave her a need to shine, be important; perhaps she would have been like that anyway. Some people are. But not you. You seem to think that your star never even got born. Don't you?'

'No,' she denied with a lofty tone that chased brief amusement across his face. 'I'm well aware of my capabilities—and limitations.'

'Are you? Then why do you always expect people to prefer your sister to yourself?'

'I don't.'

He gave a disbelieving grunt. 'Anyway, that's why she lied. She'd seen me come out of your room, and it was pretty obvious I hadn't been *cleaning it*, learning any *lines*. I'd shown her up in front of the film crew, in front of *you*, the one person she always needs to impress.'

'Impress? You make it sound as though she's jealous of me, and that's absurd!'

'No, it isn't. I hadn't given her the adulation everyone else was giving her. I was the star, you see. The important one.' His mouth twisted for a moment, before he continued, 'I'd made love to her *sister*, and that couldn't go unpunished, because, you see, I had never made love to her. And then I compounded the error. I ignored her. As, apparently, I ignored her once before— and then I walked across to speak to you...'

'Shout at me.'

'Shout, but she didn't know that, did she? And it couldn't be allowed, could it,' he asked gently, 'for the pretty sister to be ignored and the plain one not? She had an image to keep up, that she was special, important; she had to promote the lie that famous film stars found her irresistible. Especially in front of you.'

Turning so that she could see his face, recognising that there might be *some* truth in that statement, she murmured thoughtfully, 'She didn't expect me ever to ask you? See you again? And so the lie was safe?'

'Something like that. Certainly she didn't expect to see *me* again, didn't expect me to go and ask her, specifically, why she had lied. And perhaps it *was* inconceivable to her that I might, at some future date, actually look you up, want to see you. I don't think she stopped to consider what might happen if I did, just wanted to make herself appear important in your eyes.'

'But that doesn't make her important!' she exclaimed confusedly.

'No,' he agreed softly.

'That's sad.'

'What is?' he asked gently.

'Needing to shine so badly that you lie. I mean, it's not as if there was ever any need to be jealous of me... I mean, I could understand it if I were the pretty one with the enviable lifestyle...'

'You think her lifestyle is enviable, Paris?'

Glancing up, puzzled, she shook her head. 'No, not me, I told you how I felt about the film industry, but other people do. Friends, neighbours...'

'Because she promotes herself, exaggerates, wants to be envied—and because, in truth, her life isn't nearly so interesting as your own. You don't ever boast about the people you meet, the places you've been—but people who've worked with you, met you, and who also know Athena, tend to tell her how nice you are. Kind, capable, good fun... Exceptionally elegant.'

Rupert hadn't. He'd said she should be grateful that he'd even noticed her. Utterly nonplussed, not sure she believed his explanation, she just stared at him. 'Do they?' she asked, sounding almost wistful.

He smiled, nodded. 'The crew had been telling her just that before you came into the dining-room, or so Henry said. She weren't amused,' he parodied softly. 'But no one ever says that about her to you, do they?'

'No, but they say... that she's pretty, that we aren't alike...'

'And you always thought they were making comparisons, to your detriment.'

'No, not detriment,' she denied weakly. 'Just making observations. Well, she *is* pretty!'

'Yes, she is. And not very happy. The Athenas of this world always think the grass is greener somewhere else. Afraid that they might be missing something, and so they exaggerate, show off.' Turning her to face him fully, his arms linked round her back, he asked gently, 'Have we wasted enough time yet?'

'Pardon?' she asked shakily.

Releasing her, framing her confused face with warm palms, he stared down into her bewildered eyes. 'I want to kiss you,' he said softly, 'I want to hold you in my arms, and kiss you.'

Feeling almost ill, she just stared at him helplessly, moved her eyes to his mouth.

'You remember that moment in the hut? When you made me so irritated that I kissed you?'

She nodded. How could she forget?

'It was like kissing—an angel,' he said softly. 'Heavenly. Gave me one hell of a jolt. Gave you one, too, didn't it?'

She gave another cautious nod.

'And I didn't know what to do about it. Simply did not know what to do. I couldn't get it out of my mind. You'd needled me, disrupted all attempts to get into the mood for filming, concentrate; you'd made it very clear that you disliked me, and I didn't *want* to be affected by it. It was only a kiss.'

'Yes,' she agreed, almost mesmerised by his soft voice. 'Only a kiss.'

'I didn't even like you, I told myself. Didn't like you very *much*,' he corrected humorously. 'Pretended that that awareness didn't exist. And then we stopped at that funny little café, stopped to help that old lady...'

'Dragged you all in to help.'

'Not dragged,' he denied. 'We were more than willing, and so I saw a different side to you. And then, sitting in the car outside the hotel, you looked little and cold and sad...' With another of his self-mocking smiles, he added, 'And I wanted to hold you, give you a cuddle, kiss you again. You have such a marvellously sexy mouth, did you know?'

She weakly shook her head.

'A mouth just begging to be kissed.' His voice thicker, Paris's breath suspended in a tight lump in her chest, he leaned forward, just touched his mouth to hers, took his time over it, savoured the taste of her lips. 'And then,' he continued, his eyes still lingering on her mouth, 'you had too much to drink at the party, and, because I was liking you, was amused by you—and aroused by you— I insisted on escorting you to your room. We fell on your bed, and, suddenly, I wanted to make love to you. But you barely knew me, had only just begun to relax with me, allow possible friendship, and I didn't want to frighten you away.'

'I don't frighten easily,' she whispered huskily, and then scolded herself for being a fool. She had to say no, break the contact now, before it was too late, before she succumbed to foolish desires.

'I know. Now. I didn't then. And there was also the memory of your taunts, about another girl, that I supposedly seduced. And I didn't, after all, know you very well, and so I tried to be cautious...'

'You thought I might—kiss and tell?'

'It was a possibility, and so I tried to back off...'

'And I wouldn't let you.'

'Mmm. And when we woke and you were so—regretful, so mortified, at first, I thought...'

'That I *was* another with blackmail on my mind?'

'Yes, I thought I was being used.'

'And I was so full of my own embarrassment...' And then so full of anticipation. With a long sigh, she asked unexpectedly, 'Have you ever been married, Oliver?'

Obviously surprised by the change of topic, he shook his head.

'Why?'

'Because I never found who I was looking for. Sometimes I thought I had, but it always turned out to be—illusion,' he said softly. 'I'm a very cautious fellow.'

'Not always.'

'No,' he agreed, 'not always. But so many of my colleagues have married, divorced, paid vast sums in settlement, and it all seemed such a waste. Sad, and so I wanted to be sure.'

'I see.' Still staring rather helplessly at him, remembering what Henry had said, she opened her mouth, closed it and sighed. She'd got things wrong all along the line, hadn't she?

'And I wasn't *sure* about you, Paris. Awful to be so cynical, I know, but you weren't like anyone I'd ever known. And anyway, it was only a brief encounter, I kept telling myself, and, as such, to be forgotten. Only I couldn't forget it; I kept remembering your warmth, your passion—your accusations. And so I left, angry with you, and then with myself. And then I stopped to consider why. Why was I angry? I'd liked you, but it was, after all, only a temporary liaison...' A rather wry smile in his eyes, he touched his nose to hers, but didn't explain further, which left Paris prey to all sorts of doubts and fears. 'And then, when I eventually got to the studio, things had been delayed so I came to see you—and then they were un-delayed and I had to go back. Filming was going to tie me up for at least another week, and then I had to go to Africa, and that was so damnably harrowing that I didn't want to ring you, speak about it on the phone; I needed to see you face to face. And then, when I was free, I couldn't find you.'

'How did you know where I lived?'

'William.'

'Oh. And then I was ill.'

'Yes, and so it obviously wasn't the time to talk about it in any detail.'

'And then you discovered that I was pregnant,' she whispered.

'No.'

'What?' she asked, confused.

'And then I discovered that I loved you. *Then* I discovered that you were pregnant.'

Loved her?

'And I was angry—no, I was out of my mind—and so I accused you... Oh, Paris, I can't tell you how I felt. So—gutted. So I left. And now I've come back.'

'Yes.' The room was shadowy, dim, firelight flickered in his eyes masking their expression. Loved her? Had? Or did? And if it was had then she couldn't allow herself to be beguiled, persuaded, because of the baby...

He gave a funny little sigh, as though he were—disappointed? And then he moved her hair aside, touched his mouth to her nape. 'The fragrance of your skin is warmth and contentment...'

With a little shiver, she asked sadly, 'What film script is that from?'

'Book, not film,' he said softly, his breath puffing gently against her exposed nape, making her shiver more. '*A Wayward Life*. Debner. It seemed—appropriate.' Linking his arms back round her, folding her against him, he asked softly, 'Do you always make up other people's minds for them?'

Puzzled, she shook her head.

'Put words in their mouths?'

'No, of course not.'

'Then why do it to me?'

Turning her head, searching his face, trying to see the expression in his dark eyes, her own quizzical and bewildered, she denied, 'I didn't.'

'Yes, you did. You said you knew it could go nowhere, that you couldn't have my love to keep.'

'And so?'

'And so, that's putting words in my mouth, making assumptions about my feelings, my needs.'

Still staring into his eyes, her heart gave an erratic beat. 'What does that mean?' she asked carefully, her voice barely audible.

'It means that you are a fool, that you lack intuition, that you make assumptions about yourself and other people. So now *I* will tell *you*. We will get married, as soon as...'

'No...'

'Yes.'

'Oliver, you——'

'Paris, you have just confessed that you love me. Confessed it very eloquently, touchingly...'

'I did not confess it because I expected a declaration! Oliver, you aren't thinking...'

'See? There you go again, assuming you're the only one capable of making decisions...'

'No! But you can't *marry* me!'

'I can do anything I damned well choose,' he reproved, on the edge of laughter. 'I'm a famous actor, you just said so.'

'Oliver! Will you be sensible?'

'I'm being eminently sensible. We're going to get married. You are going to be my wife. And a very nice wife you will make, too. The mother of my child...'

'Oliver!' she broke in, exasperated. 'You cannot marry me!'

'When's it due, by the way?'

'August! Probably. But you cannot...' His mouth cut off the boring repetition.

When he finally allowed her to breathe, he continued musingly, 'If it's a girl, we could call her Vienna...'

'Very funny. Oliver...'

'And if it's a boy, what about Vladivostock?'

'Oliver!'

He grinned, a beautiful, boyish, happy grin. 'I forgot to wish you happy New Year.'

'That's not for days! Oliver...'

He laughed. Just threw back his head and laughed, hugged her tighter and looked down into her exasperated face. 'I *adore* you, the future Mrs Darnley.'

'Oliver... The future Mrs what?'

'Darnley.'

'Your name isn't Darke?'

'Nope. I was informed, when I first embarked on my crazy career, that Darnley wasn't sufficiently memorable. My mother was *very* cross. But I was young,' he sighed, 'eager...'

'Oliver,' she reproved darkly, 'stop playing silly beggers.'

'But I *was*!' he exclaimed in mock indignation. 'When I was discovered on the front of a knitting-pattern...'

'On the front of a *what*?'

'Knitting-pattern.'

'What were you doing on the front of a knitting-pattern?'

'Modelling a jumper, of course.' Linking his arms more comfortably round her back, he rested his nose on hers. 'When I was a student at university, to make money—holiday job. Good-looking little devil, I was... Still am, of course.' The laughter in his eyes intensified, and then he gave her a rueful grin, and suddenly sobered. 'Oh, Paris,' he exclaimed softly, 'don't you *know* how I feel about you? Haven't you *ever* known? I *adore* you, you silly girl. You make me laugh, want to hold you, protect you, and when you were so ill it nearly broke my heart. So determined to struggle on alone, so stubborn, your poor little face all white and bruised-looking... *That's* when I fell in love with you.'

'Oliver!' she protested, 'You asked me what sort of fool you were being...'

'Shh. *Asked*, hypothetical. Anyway, I already knew that I wasn't going to allow you to escape. And there was no time to talk, explain, I had already arranged to go out to the States; I needed to see your sister, get that sorted out. Then I had bloody *Rupert* in my mind! Warned myself not to jump to conclusions, and then I found out about the baby—and you hadn't *told* me. I didn't even know if it was mine!'

'I'm sorry,' she whispered, not entirely convinced she was hearing what she thought she was hearing. 'But what else could I do?'

'I know, I know,' he soothed gently. 'But there's a cold little place inside of me, and I keep thinking, if I hadn't picked up that card and read it, *would* you have ever told me? Would you have allowed me to go on thinking it was Rupert's?'

'I don't know,' she confessed unhappily. 'I've been feeling so anguished, so muddled and unhappy, and I thought it would be for the best.'

Hugging her to him, smoothing one large palm across her hair, he sighed. 'So I went for a walk, eventually calmed down, thought rationally—and realised it didn't make any difference. Whether you still loved Rupert or not, it didn't alter the way I feel. And then I decided that your having the baby made it better.'

'Better?'

'Yes, because now you would have to marry me—to protect my reputation,' he smiled.

'Oh, Oliver,' she sighed.

There was a little silence, and then he asked quietly, 'Did you love him very much, this Rupert of yours?'

Her throat aching, she shook her head. 'No. He never made me feel the way you make me feel just by looking at me, never made me feel as I wanted to feel—and when

I found out about his affair, I think I *hated* him! He said...'

'What did he say?' he prompted gently.

Hesitating, not sure it was something she wanted to share with anyone, she finally confessed, 'He said plain girls should be grateful for anything they could get, as though he'd *honoured* me,' she choked in remembered anger. 'And that I surely hadn't expected him to be *faithful*! Well, I *had*. Naïve of me perhaps, but...'

'No,' he broke in.

Startled by the tone in his voice, she turned to look at him. 'No?'

'Dear God, woman, don't you think you have the same rights as everyone else?'

'Yes, of course—and why are you sounding so angry?'

'Because I *am* angry! But it explains why you have such a bloody awful opinion of yourself!'

'I don't have an awful opinion of myself!' she exclaimed, affronted. 'I just...'

'Believed what he said!'

'Half believed,' she muttered, 'which has nothing whatever to do with what we were—er—discussing.'

'Yes, it does. I *love* you, Paris. *Need* you. Not words, not an—honour! Love, and all that goes with it. To cherish you, take care of you, be loved in return. So don't say no any more,' he pleaded gently. 'Say yes. Yes please, yes thank you, yes whatever—but yes.'

Her eyes still searching his, tears trembling on her lashes, she whispered, 'I can't.'

'You can.'

'Shouldn't, then.'

'Should. You won't have to attend glitzy parties, if that's what's worrying you. Won't have to meet egotistical idiots; you can stay at home, be a mummy. I'm in the fortunate position of being able to pick and choose parts now, do only what I want to do. We won't even need to travel, if you don't want to. Maybe I could switch to directing, theatre work...'

'Oh, Oliver, don't. I think I'm going to grizzle.'

'Say yes first. Come on, it's not so hard. You love me, don't you? Don't you?'

'Yes,' she whispered thickly.

'And you trust me, don't you?'

'Yes.' And she did trust him now, did want him to be with her always, be with him.

'Yes,' he breathed against her ear.

She sighed, had barely nodded, when he scooped her up as though she were fragile, as though she were porcelain, carried her out and up the stairs to a softly lit room that had obviously been prepared for her, and laid her gently on the bed. 'Good girl,' he approved softly. 'Now, how does this very elegant outfit undo?'

With a tremulous smile, she showed him. 'Really love me?'

'Really,' he agreed as he carefully removed her knitted top and began on the tailored trousers.

'Oh. Not because of the baby?'

'Not because of the baby.'

'A sexy mouth?'

'Very, very sexy. I'll do my own undressing; you seem to be having trouble.'

Removing her hands, she watched him and allowed hope, cautious acceptance to creep into her mind. 'It seems very extraordinary.'

'Exceptionally.'

'The famous Oliver Darke... I'm very plain.'

'As a pikestaff,' he agreed cheerfully.

'We don't know each other very well...'

'We've *always* known each other.'

Yes, despite the misunderstandings, it certainly felt that way. 'I might not mind attending *one* film première.'

'One sounds good.'

'Even appear on a magazine cover...'

'Great.'

'I might even ... Mmm, that's nice—oh, Oliver.'

He spluttered with laughter, abandoned the explorations he was making with his mouth, climbed in beside her, above her, dragged the duvet over their heads, made a nice, warm little tent, mingled his breath with hers. 'Can't have you getting cold.'

'No.' With a little shiver that had absolutely nothing to do with atmospheric conditions, she ran her palms down his warm body, halted and dragged in a deep breath. 'Oh, boy.'

'Certainly am.'

With a little giggle, she burrowed closer, moved to accommodate him, gasped, sighed—and then groaned in pleasure, clasping him so very tight when his mouth met hers.

'Is it all right?' he asked raggedly, belatedly. 'I mean, the baby and everything?'

'Yes,' she gasped.

'Thank God.' And then there was nothing to say for a while, because neither of them had the breath to say it. Not that words were needed, yet, because their bodies said it for them. Blissfully.

Cruel Legacy

One man's untimely death deprives a wife of her husband, robs a man of his job and offers someone else the chance of a lifetime...

Suicide — the only way out for Andrew Ryecart, facing crippling debt. An end to his troubles, but for those he leaves behind the problems are just beginning, as the repercussions of this most desperate of acts reach out and touch the lives of six different people — changing them forever.

Special large-format paperback edition

OCTOBER
£8.99

W★RLDWIDE

Next Month's Romances

Each month you can choose from a wide variety of romance with Mills & Boon. Below are the new titles to look out for next month, why not ask either Mills & Boon Reader Service or your Newsagent to reserve you a copy of the titles you want to buy – just tick the titles you would like and either post to Reader Service or take it to any Newsagent and ask them to order your books.

Please save me the following titles:	Please tick	✓
DANGEROUS ALLIANCE	*Helen Bianchin*	
INDECENT DECEPTION	*Lynne Graham*	
SAVAGE COURTSHIP	*Susan Napier*	
RELENTLESS FLAME	*Patricia Wilson*	
NOTHING CHANGES LOVE	*Jacqueline Baird*	
READY FOR ROMANCE	*Debbie Macomber*	
DETERMINED LADY	*Margaret Mayo*	
TEQUILA SUNRISE	*Anne Weale*	
A THORN IN PARADISE	*Cathy Williams*	
UNCHAINED DESTINIES	*Sara Wood*	
WORLDS APART	*Kay Thorpe*	
CAPTIVE IN EDEN	*Karen van der Zee*	
OLD DESIRES	*Liz Fielding*	
HEART OF THE JAGUAR	*Rebecca King*	
YESTERDAY'S VOWS	*Vanessa Grant*	
THE ALEXAKIS BRIDE	*Anne McAllister*	

If you would like to order these books in addition to your regular subscription from Mills & Boon Reader Service please send £1.90 per title to: Mills & Boon Reader Service, Freepost, P.O. Box 236, Croydon, Surrey, CR9 9EL, quote your Subscriber No:................................. (if applicable) and complete the name and address details below. Alternatively, these books are available from many local Newsagents including W H Smith, J Menzies, Martins and other paperback stockists from 11 November 1994.

Name:...

Address:...

....Post Code:.........................

To Retailer: If you would like to stock M&B books please contact your regular book/magazine wholesaler for details.

You may be mailed with offers from other reputable companies as a result of this application. If you would rather not take advantage of these opportunities please tick box. ☐